TO AND FRO

Kelsey's Journey

LT LADINO BRYSON

Renewing
Your Mind
Ink

Renewing Your Mind Ink (an imprint of Peace In The Storm Publishing, LLC)

To and Fro: Kelsey's Journey © 2021 by LT Ladino Bryson

This book is a work of fiction. Names, Characters, places, and incidents are products of the author's imagination or are used fictitiously unless otherwise indicated. Any resemblance to actual events, locales, or persons living or dead is entirely coincidental.

Although the author and publisher have made every effort to ensure the accuracy and completeness of information contained in this book, we assume no responsibility for errors, inaccuracies, omissions, or any inconsistency herein.

ISBN-13: 978-1-58441-004-1

Renewing Your Mind Ink,
a division of The Renewing Your Mind Foundation
243 East Brown Street
East Stroudsburg, PA 18301

Visit our Web site at www.PeaceInTheStormPublishing.com

In loving memory of James C. Rollins;
you taught me how to walk the walk.

Acknowledgments

Caleb and Marcus,
Thank you for sacrificing precious time, that was rightfully yours, in order for mommy to complete this book.

Unlike other types of amnesia, retrograde, anterograde, repressed memories or post-traumatic disorder, Global Amnesia is an extremely rare form which can cause a loss of memory as a defense mechanism of the brain after a traumatic event. Usually caused by a sharp blow to the head, this type of amnesia can last either short-term or long term.

Prologue

As the driver sped her shiny gold-colored Mercedes Coupe down the New Jersey Turnpike, she was so distracted by her anger that she didn't see the eighteen-wheeler in the right lane next to her. She was so preoccupied with screaming into her cell phone at the top of her lungs that she darted over into the truck's path without looking into her side mirror. It wasn't until she heard the earsplitting sound of the truck's horn, the screech of its tires and saw how close the truck was in the rearview mirror that she realized how perilous the situation was. She screams.

Even though the truck driver slammed on its brakes, the gold-colored car was hit on the right rear passenger side and immediately began to spin out of control. The female driver tried to gain control of the 34th birthday present she had bought herself a few months ago, but to no avail. In her panic, she accidentally hit the gas instead of the brakes and slid into another vehicle. The Mercedes flipped over almost instantly causing its driver to hit her head several times before the car settled on its roof on the side of the Turnpike's road.

The accident between the truck and two cars happened so suddenly that Sgt. Duncan barely had time to say, "OH MY GOD!" He was thankful that more cars had not been on the road. Normally, the turnpike was notorious for being swarmed with automobiles during rush hour. However, due to Veteran's Day, traffic was much lighter than usual, and he was able to get over safely. He called in the accident requesting emergency service vehicles as he leapt from his car and ran over to the upside-down mangled Mercedes. Inside the driver was wedged between the airbag and her seat. She was still locked in her seatbelt and her long black hair flowed freely as her body dangled upside down. Having worked as a police officer for years, Sgt. Duncan instinctively removed the driver from the vehicle, and he laid her on the gravel away from the wrecked car. The driver's beautiful features poked through the blood and soot that was smeared across her face. The sound of fire trucks and ambulances could be heard in the distance as he checked her vitals. The smell of burnt rubber and crashed metal floated through the air.

Once assessing that the driver was still breathing he felt the emergency workers, who were charging toward him, would take good care of the driver.

"Hold on help is coming. Help is coming and you are going to be fine, young lady. Just fine you hear?" Sgt. Duncan spoke as if the driver could hear him, but she was knocked out cold.

When the paramedic pushed him out of the way, Sgt. Duncan was no longer worried about the driver's safety but was more concerned about collecting the pieces of paper he saw scattered about in the car. Sgt. Duncan could now hear police sirens drawing near so he knew his time in the car would be limited. He quickly crawled inside the car, turned off the ignition, and as he gathered the evidence, he soon realized that the file folder which had his business card stapled on the outside front cover was missing. Panicked, he stuffed the pieces of paper into his pants pockets and pulled himself out of the car, buttoning up his jacket as he did so.

"Hey Sarge...what are you doing out here?" asked one of his former subordinates.

"I just turned off the ignition. Can you believe it? I was driving by when the accident occurred. I'm the one who called it in," the retired Sgt. Duncan coolly responded as he darted his eyes from side-to-side walking toward the officer.

10

"Lucky for her."

"Yeah. She appears to be still breathing. How are your wife and kids?" Sgt. Duncan asked as the manila file folder came into view about 25 feet behind the officer he was chatting with and was lying up ahead. It must have flown out the car's window.

"I can't complain."

"Good. How old is little Johnny now?"

"Just turned seven. Hey Sarge, I'm gonna go and check in with the paramedics. Don't leave okay? I need to get a statement from you."

"Sure thing. Glad I'm here to help out," Sgt. Duncan said as he moved over to the side of the road next to the high grass that lined the turnpike. Standing directly over the file folder, Sgt. Duncan bent over and tied his shoe. As he stood up he carefully kicked the folder into the grass and darted into the high brush. Sgt. Duncan then unzipped his pants and stuffed the folder inside the backside of his pants. He came walking out of the grass zipping up his fly. When the young officer saw him, Sgt. Duncan shrugged, smiled, and said, "Duty called." The young officer shook his head at the old timer and gave a hearty laugh.

Chapter One

In the Hospital

The day I opened my eyes and found myself lying in a hospital, I was horrified. First of all, I never go anywhere without a full layer of Mac cosmetics on, so the thought of my skin looking pasty against my dirty blond hair was a dreadful one. The thought of my pale blue eyes looking washed out without at least one coat of mascara frightened me more than those who saw me lying there in my weakened state. My lashes were caked together, and I could barely part them wide enough to give me a clear view of a foreign face that was peering down on me. My arms felt as if they had been poured into cement, so wiping my eyes clean was out of the question. My head was throbbing, and I had a horrible taste in my mouth as if I hadn't brushed my teeth in months. Not to mention, my jaw hurt. As I slowly opened my eyes, all I could see was some crazy lady peering down at me.

"Thank the Lord, my baby is awake!" She screeched in a high-pitched tone. "Gregory! Gregory! She's awake! Nurse, she's awake!"

This strange older woman was spitting in my face as she shouted and jumped up and down. Her voluptuous top frame would surely black both of her eyes if she jumped too high. But more importantly, her loud, shrilly voice was making my headache worsen. Though my eyes felt swollen, my mouth was working just fine.

"Ma'am, would you mind taking it down a notch, please? Or at least can you get the nurse?"

I tried not to sound angry, but actually, I was pissed that someone let this strange woman in my room. She kept shouting something over and over, and I had to tune her out completely in order to yell louder than her.

"HELP! SECURITY! HELP ME PLEASE!" Thank God, a tall man ran into the room and pushed the crazy lady away from my bed.

"How do you feel, Kelsey?" he said gently.

"What kind of hospital are you running here where strange people can just walk into your room and disturb you as they please? Lady, I'm in a hospital. I'm obliviously sick and trying to rest here, so will you please leave my room so I can rest? Are you my doctor?" I babbled.

"Doctor? Uhh…no, I'm not, I—"

"Well, would you be a dear and call the nurse, doctor, or information for all I care. I need some answers and painkillers immediately. My head is killing me." No one moved. They just kept looking at me like I was speaking a foreign language.

"I'll get the nurse. She's talking crazy. Help us, she's awake! Will somebody get in here quick?" The crazy lady left the room.

"Thank goodness she finally left. So, who are you? A security guard? A technician? Why am I in the hospital?" I asked.

"I'm none of the above and you are in the hospital because you had a really bad car accident a few days ago?" This stranger or stalker or whoever he was, had the nerve to sit on my bed as he was talking.

"Do you mind?"

"Oh, sorry."

"I don't know what you want, but I don't think I have anything for you to steal, so why don't you just get out of my room quickly before I start screaming again," I threatened.

"What is wrong with you?" the stranger asked looking as if he just saw a ghost. "Nurse! Where's Dr. Jamie Hyman? I need help in here. Nurse!" he shouted as he exited the room.

What a nightmare. What's with all of the crazy people, and why am I in a hospital where there is no staff around? I don't deserve this drama or this headache. The pain in my head made me squint my eyes as I looked around the room to see if the name of the hospital were on anything so I could try and figure out where the heck I was. To my left there was some kind of large equipment of some kind with a sticker on it that read: *Property of Clay Memorial Hospital Wellington, NJ.* Mental note: Get transferred out of this crazy place immediately!

As I started to look around the room, I could see they must have stuck me in the smallest room imaginable. As I turned my head, I could hear groaning sounds coming from across the room. I tried to focus for a moment, but with blurred vision, I could only see that there was another person in the room with me. Glimpses of her smooth, tan skin color could be seen between the tubes throughout her nose and arms. She had bandages around her head, and you could tell the sheets were too short for her long legs because her feet stuck out from under them. She wiggled her dirty left foot at me as a type of greeting. I rolled my eyes back in my head refusing to respond to her.

"Oh, my goodness! I must be poor," I stated loudly, "for them to put me in a county facility, in a room with another person, and in a place where the sheets don't even cover you properly!"

As I continued to scan the room, I noticed a small area to my right that had a window. There was a chair underneath it, and a medium-sized TV bolted to the ceiling. I could never understand why a hospital would bolt a heavy TV right above a patient or whatever guest that might be sitting in that chair. What if it fell on them? That's a lawsuit ready to happen. Then there was the lady across from me, and at the opposite end of the room was a tiny closet that looked big enough to hold a small clutch purse. Oh, my goodness!

Where is my purse? I tried to sit up so that I could move over to the closet, but the sharp pain in my head returned, forcing me to lie back down quickly. I was left staring up at the ugly oatmeal-colored ceiling for a moment or two.

When I felt strong enough, I decided to finish giving the room a once over and noticed the monitors to my left were connected to my left arm, which was being intravenously fed through roads of tendon-like tubes. I wish I could figure out which one had the painkillers. I desperately needed to up my dosage. What is going on? Still, no nurse or doctor. I turned my head over to the right and saw all kinds of flowers and cards on the nightstand beside my bed. That's nice. I don't know how I missed them the first time I scanned the room.

There were so many of them you would have thought I was dying. I was just about to scream my lungs out when the crazy lady and a nurse ran into my room.

"Nurse, please find me some painkillers, my head is killing me! You are the nurse, right? I keep getting strange people walking in and out of my room. What's she doing back here? Thanks for getting the nurse, ma'am; now can I get some privacy, please?" I was in a lot of pain. "Well, semi-privacy, since I'm stuck in this tiny room with her."

The crazy woman didn't budge but she slowly looked over her shoulder at the other woman and stared at her for a moment. Oh my gosh! I didn't think about it until now, but maybe the crazy lady was a friend or family to the other woman in the room. They had to be related. Her smooth tanned skin matched the woman's laying in the bed. Instead of tending to the other patient, for some reason, she just kept staring at me.

"No, Kelsey, I'm not a nurse. I'm Dr. Jamie Hyman."

"Thank goodness. and thanks again, ma'am, for getting the doctor for me. What's wrong with me, and why didn't they put me in a private room?"

"Kelsey, do you know what day it is?" the doctor asked as she checked my tubes.

"No. Ka-who? What did you just call me?"

"Kelsey. That's your name. Don't you remember?" she questioned.

"Kelsey? What kind of name is Kelsey? Who would name their daughter Kelsey? I sound like a poodle. I think you got my chart mixed up with hers," I stated as I darted my eyes in the direction of the patient across the room.

"Gregory! Gregory, get in here!" The strange woman ran out of the room as if she now saw a ghost.

"No, I am quite sure that your name is Kelsey."

"What happened to me?"

"You were in a horrible accident on the turnpike a couple of days ago. You have been unconscious since they brought you in. Your family has been worried sick about you, and so have I. But it's good to see that you have come out of it. Your vital signs are all reading well."

"Well then, why do I feel as if I were hit by a truck?"

"Ironically, Kelsey, you were."

"Huh?"

"You were driving along the New Jersey Turnpike, and as you were changing lanes trying to pull over onto the side, a truck hit you causing your car to flip over."

"OUCH!"

"You are very blessed to be alive right now and we are all very thankful."

"You keep referring to other people, who are the "all" you keep referring to?"

"Well, your family and me. Don't you know who I am?"

"Yeah, you just said you're Dr. Jamie Hyman."

"Interesting."

"What?"

"Kelsey, do you remember ever seeing me before today?"

"No."

"Are you sure?"

"Yes. Should I not be sure?"

"Well, it is a little odd since we have been friends for over two decades."

"You and me? Really?" I asked as I gave her a quick once over. She was medium height with hazel eyes and olive skin. She had long dark hair and appeared to look too young to be a doctor. I don't care what this woman thinks, I never saw her before in my life.

Chapter Two

Dr. Jamie

As she walked out of the room, Dr. Jamie Hyman was really scared. She had known Kelsey since they met in junior high almost twenty years ago. Tears began to well up in her eyes. She couldn't remember a time that they had gone two days without speaking. Kelsey had been more than a best friend but a sister to her all of these years. And now her sister, the Thelma to her Louise, couldn't even remember her face. The pain was unbearable. She pushed past Gregory and Mrs. Smith and rushed towards the bathroom.

"Jamie, what is wrong with my wife?" Gregory shouted as the door closed behind her.

Searching for an empty stall, she forced the door open quickly, grabbed her long hair, bent over the bowl, and dry heaved into the water. She felt faint. Staring into the toilet bowl filled with a colorless liquid, she knew she had to pull herself together—if for nothing else, for Kelsey.

"Baby, are you okay?" Mrs. Smith asked concerned as she entered the bathroom. Jamie had been like a daughter to her all these years. Mrs. Smith couldn't remember a time that the two girls had been separated. Even in college, though they had different career goals and went to separate schools, they shared an apartment mid-distance from Seton Hall and Rutgers University. They have always been the best of friends.

"I'll be alright, Mom," Jamie answered.

"Jamie, you've got to give it to us straight. What's wrong with my child? She acts as if she doesn't know us."

"She doesn't." With that, Jamie flushed the toilet and began to clean herself up. Staring into the mirror as the faucet ran warm water, memories started to flood Jamie's mind as she prepared for the task at hand.

Jamie would never forget the day she first met Kelsey. How could she? She was the skinniest thing she had ever seen—tall and just plain skinny; a beanpole to be exact. She had a huge warm smile, caramel wide eyes with thick lashes, long brown hair like her own and the loudest mouth she had ever heard. You could hear the girl from across the quad laughing and talking back to a group of boys who were trying to poke fun at her physique. Her laugh was so infectious that it aroused the curiosity of the group of kids that Jamie was with, and they all headed over to the bunch to see what was so funny.

Moments before, there was a group of jocks sitting together on a bench, and a kid named Sean made fun of Kelsey by drawing a picture of her. The picture consisted of just one straight line on a sheet of crisp white paper.

"This is a picture of Kelsey," he said as he showed it to about ten football players and their girlfriends as Kelsey walked by. Kelsey couldn't help but laugh with them. Why fight it? She knew she was skinny, and there was nothing that she could do about it.

"Oh yeah? Well, let me draw a picture of you, Sean," Kelsey smirked. Drawing a crowd with her loud voice, she took the picture that Sean made of her and started to draw on the back. With her lips pursed, she began to scribble quickly. Jamie had heard of the caliber of Kelsey's comedic nature and stood waiting in anticipation for her response. Finally, with high dramatics, Kelsey turned the picture around to reveal the crisp white blank page.

"TA-DA! Here's Sean!"

We all fell out in vicious howls. Then taking a red pen, Kelsey scribbled onto the paper wildly.

"And this is Sean after I embarrass him!" she cracked.

More roaring laughs. Sean stormed off mad and red-faced. For a brief moment, Sean had forgotten that he was an albino.

That was the kind of person Kelsey was…it was as if she was always playing chess in her mind. Quick-witted, smart, funny, and adventurous. She was the kind of person most wanted to be around or to live vicariously through. But not me. Even vicariously, I couldn't keep up with Kelsey. Never could and never wanted to; I was the turtle, and she was the hare. I guess that's what made us such great friends. There was never any competition between us, just great moments. Kelsey was there with me to share all of my teenage secrets and all of my "firsts." Kelsey set up my first date, or double date, to be exact. It was so horrible! I can't even begin to explain it, so I won't.

She was there for my first love, my first heartbreak, and my first marriage. Well, my one and only marriage. Kelsey insists that I should remain hopeful, so I always refer to it as my "first marriage."

Being an only child, the Smiths sort of adopted me. I never had a lonely day after that autumn day in the quad during the second month of school. After Sean stormed off, mutual friends introduced us, and we became instant friends. I was her voice of reason and she was my pillar of strength. I was the Maid of Honor at her wedding, and she the my Matron of Honor at mine. I am the godmother to her two beautiful boys, and she was right by my side when I had my miscarriage. She was even there the day I found out that my husband was Mr. Wrong. I was so upset that I had her assistant pull her out of an important meeting that took her three weeks to prepare.

Being a true friend, Kelsey didn't think twice about putting me first as she took the call. I immediately gave her an update about Steven and how I had moved out from the house we shared. I was blubbering so hard from a broken heart, going on and on about things that I didn't hear Kelsey excuse herself from the meeting explaining that she needed to attend to a family emergency. She quietly drove over to my hotel room. When she got off the phone with her, I thought she returned to her meeting. I sat looking around the room ready to throw myself a pity party. Unbeknownst to me she was right outside my hotel room waiting for me to answer the door. I opened the door, and there was Kelsey standing in front of me with open arms.

"It looks like you need a big hug," she lovingly stated as she scooped me up into her arms.

Like I said, there has never been a day in my life that I have ever felt lonely since Kelsey has been around. Until now.

"Jamie, baby, you don't look so good. Do you need a doctor?" Mom asked.

I couldn't speak. I just pushed past her, back into the stall I went, only this time my lunch came up.

For a moment, Jamie thought she was really going to need a doctor, but she just needed a release. She actually felt better, and now she had to prepare herself to tell the family about Kelsey's condition. Kerri-Claire, as usual, was on stage making a big deal about Jamie throwing up.

"Child, what's wrong with you? Are you having morning sickness? Are you anorexic, bulimic, or whatever it's called?"

"No, Mom. I just needed to release some stress. I'll be fine. Don't you worry about me, Mom. Let's go find Gregory. I need to speak with you both about Kelsey's condition," I replied opening the door for her.

Down the hall, Gregory was sitting patiently waiting for us. His large brown eyes were strained, and his forehead wrinkled. The way he was wringing his fingers showed he was truly concerned. As he saw us coming towards him, he stood up.

"Jamie, what's wrong with her? She's freaking me out. She keeps talking to me as if she has no idea who I am. She even thinks there's another patient in the room with her."

"Jamie, what kind of medicine is she on?" Mom added.

"Guys, hold up. We all need to calm down because this is a very serious matter. It seems as if Kelsey has amnesia," I blurted out.

"What?"

"Oh, Lord, help me," Mom said dramatically.

"Calm down! I don't know how serious it is. It may just be that she is a little foggy from waking up or it could be more serious. Whatever the case may be, we all have to be extremely supportive of each other and Kelsey."

"Are you telling me that my wife has no recollection of who she is and who we are because of the accident?"

"Gregory, she didn't even know her name was Kelsey, and she doesn't recognize any of us. I don't know how severe her case is, only time will tell. She was in a serious accident and suffered extensive injuries to the head. It is very likely that she lost her memory temporarily, or she may not regain it at all."

"Do you mean that this accident has caused her to lose over thirty years of memories? Us, our marriage, our children…"

"Those poor babies!" Mom started to weep.

"If we want her to get better, we must calm down. Again, I don't , and won't know the extent of her injuries until we can confirm a diagnosis after extensive testing. With some tests and a couple of opinions from a couple of specialists, we might be able to understand what is going on in Kelsey's brain. I'm a therapist, so I cannot give you a full understanding of what damage has been done. For right now, I think it would be helpful if we all go into the room and introduce ourselves. We must not inundate her with information, nor push her too quickly, or she may become hostile towards us."

"What else is new?" Mom grumbled under her breath.

"Mom, this is serious. I have seen cases where a person never regained their memory and had to literally start a new life. They had to relearn themselves, their emotions, their profession, and everyone around them. The accident has caused Kelsey's brain to shut down, and I want to make sure we are there to support her so that it doesn't shut down permanently. Worst case scenario, Kelsey's brain may be acting similar to a computer that is no longer functioning correctly. Once the computer is restored to its original state, it will work fine. However, all of the programs would have to be reinstalled. Kelsey is experiencing the same thing."

"Do you mean that she has to learn how to redo everything that she has learned in her life? Like eating and stuff?" Mom questioned.

"No, like a computer, the brain knows how to function in its original state when you purchase sans all of the programs you have stored in its memory. I'm hoping that Kelsey will be able to recognize things she has already learned and can do naturally. It's just she may have no recognition of anyone or all of the experiences that have been stored in her memory. Understand?"

"I think so," Gregory answered.

"Now let's go back inside," I said as I stopped briefly, took a deep breath, smiled, and lead Gregory and Mom into Kelsey's room.

As the three walked back into the room, Kelsey was lying in her bed with her eyes closed feeling the effects of the medicine kicking in. The nurse on duty gave a quick smile as she exited. Gregory was moving towards her bed and Jamie had to tap his arm to get his attention. Shaking my head "No," he recoiled and let Jamie move closer to Kelsey.

"Kelsey, its Jamie."

"Who?" she asked with her eyes closed.

"Dr. Jamie Hyman."

"Hi, Dr. Jamie," she said as she opened her eyes smiling, dazed from the morphine. But her smile turned quickly into concern when she saw Gregory and Mrs. Smith.

"What are these strangers still doing here?"

"Kelsey, you've had a rough journey, and you must be tired, but these aren't strangers. Kelsey, this is your husband, Gregory Pritchard."

Kelsey stared at the two of them in sheer and utter disgust. Finally, she spoke to Gregory.

"You're my husband?" she said, looking Gregory up and down.

"Yes, I am, and I love you very much, Kels."

"Are we poor?" she asked in a groggy tone.

"Why would you ask a question like that?"

"Because I'm trying to figure out why I have to share a room with another patient," she whispered loudly as if not to let the woman in the other bed hear her. Gregory didn't miss a beat.

"Kelsey, that is your reflection in the mirrored door that leads to the bathroom. Sweetie, you *are* in a private room."

Accepting the fact that she was staring at her own reflection, Kelsey could, for the first time, clearly see just how many tubes were actually in her arm. She realized that her head was wrapped in gauze and that she had tubes in her nose. The medicine was starting to take affect and she was getting really sleepy. Kerri-Claire came pushing from behind, passing Gregory and Jamie to get her two cents in.

"Kelsey, baby, I am your mother. Surely you remember me?"

Kelsey just stared at her with drowsy eyes, barely able to keep them open.

She whispered before passing out, "Wow, I'm black!"

That was the way I was introduced to my husband, my mom, my supposed best friend, and not to mention myself. It's hard to explain what it felt like to be inside of a body, staring at a face, and unable to recognize, well, "me." Though I have grown used to this face and body, I sometimes find myself taking a closer gaze at my features and curves, not able to believe that this body fits my brain. When I woke up in the hospital the next day from my drug-induced slumber, I kept peering into the large-mirrored door across from my bed, trying to search my own eyes; sorting through the black and blue marks and the flesh peeking out from underneath the bandages, and looking for any expression that would activate my memory.

In the months after my accident, I spent numerous days plowing through pictures from my childhood and adult life. I even had the opportunity to meet numerous family members and friends, only to draw a complete blank regarding our association and/or times together. I've spent many nights wrestling with the fact that my brain has given up on me. And many nights frustrated because I am unable to sleep at all.

Chapter Three

I Just Want to Sleep!

I'm beginning to despise anyone who is able to get a good night's sleep. Lord, what I wouldn't do for just one night where I can effortlessly snuggle up in a warm cozy bed and just doze off into nothing. That's right, nothing. Even more, I would love to wake up one morning without the sound of my alarm clock piercing my ears. Wake up and not have to beg my husband to give me fifteen more minutes. I'd kill for a chance to sleep so peaceful that I wouldn't mind when my kids run in my room begging for "fruit snacks" first thing in the morning. I'd do anything for a chance to fall into a dreamless state of slumber.

But that in itself is a dream. They say God gives sleep to those He loves. Well, He must be really mad at me because no matter how much I fight to get some rest almost every night I drift off into the same backdrop of a cold and large wooded area. Night after night, I'm wandering, running in and out dizzily past trees whose leaves hibernate for a season. They stand so high above me that when I look up I feel like I am an ant crawling on the inside of a coffin. They mock me no matter which way I turn. They look and feel lifeless. Their bark is a grayish color of gloom and they irk me with their expressionless stares.

In this dream, its winter. I'm freezing, and I think I'm scared. I'm quite sure that I'm definitely confused. I'm always tired and desperately longing to get to my destination. Where that is I don't know. The sky is white and cold but bright, nonetheless. The sky is so blinding in certain areas it seems as if the light was trying to warn me not to go in a particular direction. I don't know how long I've been stuck in this woodland hellhole, but I know that I just want to walk to the other side. It's like a joke: "Why did the pretentious, frustrated, 30-something, wife and mother of two crosses the woods?" I don't know what triggered my journey, but I am certain that promises of hope, love, and bliss await me on the other side.

"What's that?" I whispered. I'm standing so still you'd think I was a deer trying to discern what my next move should be and praying that I won't become venison. I can hear movement coming from up ahead to my far left. Something was definitely out there. I stood still for a moment or two, holding my breath until the rustling leaves stopped. Whew! Though I didn't see it, I could only presume it must have been a small animal. Whatever it was, it was gone now.

As I continued to walk, the leaves crushing under my feet reminded me of a childhood photo taken of me playing on the lawn in my grandfather's front yard. If I weren't so distracted with surviving, I would have stopped and meditated on that thought for a moment. Birds linger high above me, calling to each other as if to report my every move.

I don't have any gloves on, and my hands are so cold. My ears are stinging from the frozen air, and what seemed like a half-hour walk has turned into many days. Or should I say many nights? I was hungry and I silently began to cry. I feel abandoned. My tears were turning into laughter because it was no use getting mad. No matter what I did, it was the same ole thing; I always end up back here when I slept.

Night after night, I tirelessly toss and turn, and no matter how many times I woke up during the middle of the night, I always fell back into the trance of the woods. Those darn trees just keep looming over me. Sometimes I'm positioned deeper into the woods. Other times, I'm close to the edge of the woods and am able to hear the faint sounds of civilization, maybe a highway or campsite but I'm never able to go near it; I'm always stuck in this nature hellhole.

I truly know what it feels like for a mouse to be ensnared in a maze. As I took a moment to catch my breath, I remember seeing an open end of a tree trunk where wild mushrooms were growing out of it and came to the realization that I'd circled the same area for the fifth time tonight. I'm pissed! The trees were starting to talk to me.

"Hey there! Did you miss me?" As I turn around to get my bearings, they shout to me, "Hey you! Where do you think you're going?" They taunt me as I continued to go around and around in circles.

"Okay, stop, relax, and concentrate. Try going northeast instead of northwest this time," I say as calmly as I can, trying to ignore the trees. I can't stand being lost.

"I just want to get to the other side," I screamed in a crackling shout that echoed between the hollow foliage. I missed being in a comfort zone. My home. The love of my children. Heck, I'd settle for the painful things right about now. Anything would be better than this. Breathing a little heavier now, I could see the frosty atmosphere creating a train of cold air beneath my nostrils. My eyes were tearing up, but I refused to cry again.

"This really doesn't make any sense," I grumbled beneath my breath. "If you love me so much, how can you abandon me out here in the cold every night to fend for myself?"

This isn't fair. Nevertheless, who said love was? Why is it whenever you need to be taught something, your loved ones choose "tough love?" What about *soft* love? I'm a smart, kind, and attentive human being. Soft love might suit me well. The thought of growing past "tough love" and experiencing change can sometimes be too overwhelming for me. I guess I get scared of all of the possibilities of maturation. What if I fail, or what if others fail me? What if I make the wrong choices again or continue to let my pride guide me through every situation? What if I break stride with my goals, or even worse, give up hope? What would happen if I died trying only to prove that I was destined to be a failure all the while? Even more so, what if I simply

27

give in and let all of the negative thoughts that tend to consume me win? I can't stand to lose. Lose out on all of the hope stored in me somewhere or that's waiting for me if I can just hold on a little longer. I can't touch it, but I know it's there waiting to break free and lift me up to a higher level. Waiting to pull me out of all of the doubt so I can hold my head up high. Right now, I wish that hope would get me out of the woods every night.

Sometimes I'm wandering around in here and I talk to myself about things I don't even know. Or can't remember. All I know is that I have something to say swelling up in me, but my voice is paralyzed from my shame. Shame of what, I can't be sure. Sadly, I'm 30ish and can't even remember turning thirty, but I can remember the year I turned one…

Chapter Four

One Year Old

When I turned one year old, I can remember standing in the midst of my birthday party not understanding why everybody was making such a big fuss over me. Everyone was acting as if they never saw me before. I was extremely annoyed. But what's new? To hear everyone tell it, I'm always annoyed. Stop taking pictures! No, I don't want any cake or your congratulatory hugs. I just want to be left alone to reflect on the year that has just passed. Okay, there is the gift factor. Hum, now that's something I could be tempted with. Who doesn't like to receive gifts?

Nevertheless, what can anyone buy me that's gonna replace the time I've lost? And I've lost so much time. There were so many cameras snapping and people waving their "hellos" that I felt dizzy. The way they were all staring at me, you'd think I was somebody important, some freakish circus act or an animal in the zoo. Nope, it's just little ole me standing before you in all my glory. What's wrong with them? Am I here to be your entertainment? I could really use a tall Dirty White Mother right now but I'm afraid to mix an alcoholic drink made of Kahlua, crème, and coffee with the glass of white wine I had earlier.

"This is gonna be a great year for you, I just know it."

"What do you want to accomplish by your second birthday?"

"Doing anything special tonight?" *Yeah, I'll be stuck in the woods like I was last night, stupid!*

"How does it feel to be a year old again?" *Again? I don't remember what if felt like the first time. What a dumb question and to think they are my family!*

"Kelly?"

"Kayla?"

My mom must have called me a couple of times before I recognized she was talking to me. She finally caught my attention and repeated my name again.

"Kelsey, are you okay dear? Are you tired? You look tired," she asked worried.

"No, Mom, I'm fine, just a little overwhelmed," I answered.

Kelsey. My name is Kelsey. Why me? When I hear people calling me, I still cannot believe my mom gave me that name. How did I get stuck with such a prissy and uptight name like Kelsey? Me of all people who is so into names and their meanings. Seriously, I mean I'm into names like some people are into astrology. I love the idea of trying to figure out what the heck parents were thinking when they decided to put an identity on a child that would be with them for their natural lives. I even purchased this book with over 20,000 names and their meanings that I carry around with me highlighting all the names I know, and when I meet new people, I look up their name's meaning. You can tell a lot about a person by their name.

Some names are prophetic, allowing you to grow into your destiny. Some so poetic you enjoy saying them over and over again, like Angel, Faith, Destiny, or Grace. Other names reflect the acid trip your parents were on or phases they were going through like Star, Ichabod, and Loyser (too close to "loser") or Lexus—as in the car. Some names are so ghetto that you probably wouldn't be able to read them, so why even bother to mention them. I'll never understand why in the world some people can match great names for their dogs but insist on creating, adding, or subtracting syllables to create concoctions young kids will have a field day making fun of. Weird names nobody can pronounce causing a seemingly normal person to get an attitude when you mispronounce them.

For instance, there was a lady in my gynecologist's office who got mad at a few of us when she proudly announced she was going to name her daughter Morhan pronounced like *more-hahn*. Naturally, I pointed out that Morhan, her precious little girl, would soon become "moron" once she hit school age. Heck, I'd even be first in line to call the girl and her mother morons if she went through with giving her child that name and politely told the woman so. She got pissed and stormed out of the waiting area. Whatever. Sometimes the truth hurts.

One of my mother's friends made up such a ridiculous concoction of a name for her daughter that no one can pronounce it. I think her name was Le Tia. Pronounce "la-tie-yah" but read like "la-tee-ha." Not to mention, it was two words with a capital "L and T." Anyway, though it's a pretty name, it's just too hard to remember, so this pretty successful woman had to reduce herself to initials so that she could properly do business without being at her wits end trying to get people to pronounce her name correctly. What's worse is that her husband can only grunt "L" whenever he beckons her. Man, how lazy can you get?

I can't stand transitional names like Ritchie, Richard, Rich, Dick, and Dickey. Pick a name! I loathe Jr., Sr., or IIIs and IVs—sorry that your mother refused to give you an identity of your own. The kid will grow up spending all his life trying to live up to someone else's name, and that's just sad. I'm a firm believer that there are just some fights a woman should automatically win. If you carry the child, you should have the right to name the child. Simply put, and end of discussion.

I love names that have profound meanings. Names that make you think. Ever notice how horrible it is to have a name on a dog that doesn't fit the breed or the dog's personality. I believe it's the same with people. Kelsey Smith-Pritchard; as I said, my name sounds too prissy. I wish my mother had named me Kayla instead; it means *pure*. Imagine being named after such a strong and calming adjective like *pure*. Makes you feel safe, doesn't it? You can trust pure because there's nothing to hide in it. But that would be really stupid naming me pure, especially when I'm a mutt. My lineage is so mixed up it runs from north to south and back again. Kelsey means *island*. Some people hear the word *island*, and images of white sandy beaches are conjured up in their heads along with thoughts of paradise, peace, or tropical adventures; or at least that's what my husband Gregory sees. I'm just the opposite. I hear the word island and immediately think, yep that's me. Isolated and detached from the rest of the world. How apropos. My mother said my skin complexion reminded her of the warm tropical colors of the Caribbean, but looking at my baby pictures, I always thought I looked more like a papoose.

I hear the name Kelsey and images of a pristinely ruffle dress little girl with long ponytails and big pink ribbons comes to mind; the kind of girl who would never jump into a puddle of mud; the kind of girl who will only play dress up. I say this because that's what I looked like in one of my childhood photos. Not that there's anything wrong with being a girly-girl, but that's not my style and I would never do that to my daughter, if I had one. I wonder…was I this negative before my episode?

At first, I thought it was kind of cool to have a nervous breakdown, amnesia, or whatever you want to call it. A lapse is a time for healing and a chance to get some much-needed rest or to make a fresh start in life. It would be a chance to rediscover my relationship with my husband and learn to love my kids all over again. Funny, but I don't know if I ever loved my husband or not. Sounds cold, I know, but how can I be sure? With some of the things he constantly does that completely irks me, I can't believe we actually got married in the first place. I swear sometimes he gets on my last nerve.

I have been diagnosed with a hysterical form of global amnesia. In a nutshell, it's the most severe there is. Though my birth certificate states that I am 35, I can only recall the last year of my life. Imagine being able to forget about all the pain and mistakes you made in life and start anew. I guess it's kind of like being reborn as an adult—a chance to have a clean slate. Everyone treats you special and showers you with love and everything becomes brand new to you. But soon, the kindness starts to wear off, and people make you feel like you must work to try to remember who you were, what you felt, and who they are, so everyone can move forward.

I try not to feel bad for myself since I'm no different than anyone else. I'm simply taking a break from things so I can reprocess them. Who could ask for more? What's the matter with soaking up a little love for a while? Why do I have to rush and be what my mind doesn't want me to be anymore? Can't I just move forward as I am?

That's what I used to think until some things just didn't make any sense. Even though I cannot put my finger on it, I can sense that things are a little off. So now I'm obsessed with finding out the truth without relying on what people tell me. Sure, there are times it becomes frustrating that I can't remember who I was, where I came from, or even the birth of my two children. That must sound frightening to some people, but it's the truth. I have no recollection of their baby smell, their tiny little bodies as I changed their diapers, their first steps, or their first day of school. I can't even recall the sound of their laughter or the sound of their cries. I've totally erased what some would consider being the joy of parenting. The connection between parent and child. The memories of them altogether.

When you have an episode like mine, each year after is celebrated as your birthday. That's why I am stuck here today in the middle of all of this. If nothing else, by my 2nd birthday, I just want to really be confident again in my ability to change and not rely on others trying to put the pieces together for me. I am hopeful that I will be able to regain my memory or at least some part of it. Until then…I'm stuck here with all of them.

Chapter Five

My Mom

Sometimes I feel as if I have never really existed. Even to myself. Does that make sense? I mean, I know that I was here to everyone that I know: my kids, family members, clients, friends, and husband, but not to the brain inside my head. I've combed through countless photo albums as if I were looking at someone else's life, completely detached from the face that was reflected back at me. Though my eyes were full of life and my smile was broad, underneath it all, my reflection appeared to be extremely cold to me. I would sit with my husband who spoke about our life together as if it were the best of times. But it didn't read that way to me. Even through the smiles and giggles capture in the photo prints, my strong personality was overpowering. I could tell by the look in my eyes I had to always be in charge of my environment, everyone, and everything around me. I was either a natural-born leader or a control freak. This was evident even in my baby pictures: I knew had it going on. The spotlight continually shone in my direction and I ate it up.

I'm almost surprised that I was never interested in drama or the arts because from what I hear, I would have been a natural. Dr. Jamie says I get that part of my personality from my mother. Though I don't feel the need of being in the spotlight today, I guess my illness has somehow put me there. The hardest thing to get used to is my mother. In the year and a half that I have known her, it takes everything that I have to try to love her. I know that must sound horrible, but it's the God's honest truth. I can't put my finger on it, but there is a level of tension that engulfs me when I'm around her. Maybe it's because we both have strong personalities or are extremely opinionated, but it always feels as if we are trying to outdo each other. She'll say one thing, and then I focus all of my energy on trying to prove her wrong so that I appear to be superior in intellect. Don't get me wrong, Ms. Kerri-Claire Smith is no slouch when it comes to being book or street-smart. I'm just saying that what she has put her energy into all of these years has not accomplished much for her, in my opinion. She lives in the realm of a quite comfortable existence.

Kerri-Claire Rollins was 20 years old when she had me. I was the product of an amorous love affair between my mom and dad, Jay Smith. I'm told they married shortly after my birth, but my dad, who worked for the post office, died when I was only two years old. I, of course, have no recollection of him at all. It's hard to believe that a woman who was so in love with a man, as my mother claims to have been with my father, that there are no pictures to account for his existence. Not even one. Being that I have no memory of him, it would have been helpful to see a picture of the two of us together. However, there is no record that he even knew me (or her for that matter). There are no wedding pictures, vacation pictures, not even photos of them at family functions or holidays. This is extremely odd for my snap-happy, picture taking family. Even though I'm an only child, I'm told that our large family was a tight knit circle of cousins, aunts, and uncles. I had a chance to meet a few aunts on my mom's side, but it appears as if my mom and my dad's side of the family don't speak.

That is what is so unnerving. There are too many inconsistencies regarding my father. When I ask my mom about my father, I am always told what I believe are tall tales of an undeniably loving relationship between the two. Where is the proof?

"Your dad was such an amazing man. Sweet and gentle. Strong and well respected," she closed her eyes and continued as if she were drawing a clear picture of him.

"How I loved him and how he cared for me. He was so handsome, tall with broad shoulders, full lips, and hazel eyes with long dreamy lashes. You've got his forehead and height, Kelsey. I miss him so much that sometimes it makes me want to cry," she would state in a calm voice.

"Mom, did you ever find the box with the photo albums of your wedding pictures? I would love to see how beautiful you looked on your wedding day," I asked watching her body language shift uncomfortably.

"I was a nursing student before I had you, and Jay worked for the post office. We had it all. Once we got married, we moved out of his parent's house and into a small apartment on Donner Street, five miles from downtown New Orleans. We lived there for a year and a half and had been saving up to buy a house when your dad died in a car crash," she finished. "That's when I moved back here to New Jersey to be closer to my family."

"Mom, did you find the photos or not?"

She always tried to skirt the issue whenever I brought up the photo album. I could understand her putting them away if she got remarried, but she never did. From what I can tell, my mother engaged in another love affair since my father. For someone who always thought often of the love of her life, isn't it odd that she didn't have one photo of him in plain view? My mom is well known for always having a camera on her at all times since the day I was born. She even admits that herself. So why haven't any photos of my dad surfaced? What is she hiding?

"No, I haven't been able to locate that box yet. I'll let you know as soon as I find it. You know, Gregory reminds me of my Jay. He acts just like him. Kelsey, you got yourself a good man. You better make sure you treat him right and stop being so hard on him, dear."

It's been the same response every time. Divert talking about my father when the pressure is on and substitute Gregory into the conversation. If my dad is anything like Gregory, then Mom should be telling tales of how much my dad smothered her.

I hate to admit it, but it always feels as if my mom is always trying to impress me. We never have any conversations where she let down her guard and just unloads her emotions, and I don't feel comfortable talking about things close to my heart with her either. She has told me on numerous occasions how much she loves me, yet her actions and body language tell a different story. Everything she did seemed forced—every gesture and every conversation. Everything she did was very mechanical, except when she is being overly dramatic. I don't care what this woman tells me, I suspect that we were never very close. We've had so many uncomfortable conversations and awkward silences that you'd think we've spent most of our time together stuck in an elevator after one of us had farted.

After all of this time, I still can't put my finger on it, but something is just not right. Whenever I question her about it, she tries to make me feel as if I'm paranoid.

"Was I adopted?" I asked.

"You're kidding, right?" Mom asked. "How could you look in a mirror and ask that question with a straight face? Are you feeling alright, honey?"

She was right. I was the spitting image of my mom, only 20 years younger. Though I didn't share her voluptuous body shape, we both had long, dark thick hair, almond-shaped eyes, and smooth skin. With our heart shaped faces, long eyelashes, and full lips, we look more like sisters than mother and daughter. I have been told that I also have a lot of her mannerisms, which to me is a scary thought.

It's not scary that we look alike—I think my mom is beautiful, but there's something deep within her that can be intensely peculiar. It's like her name, Kerri-Claire. She was named after both of her grandmothers. Kerri, after my grandmother's mother, means dark and mysterious, while Claire, after my grandfather's mother means bright and clear. Both names contradict each other, and somehow the name reflects her personality. She's an amazing grandmother. However, with me, she's always fumbling for the right words to say, and tends to avoid questions. To hear everyone else tell it, it's my imagination. I've asked Dr. Jamie what the relationship between my mother and I was really like on several occasions during our therapy sessions, but she would never give me any insight on the matter.

"Why don't you tell me anything about my mother?" "It's not my place, Kelsey."

"Isn't it your place to want me to get better?"

"I just think it would be better for you to remember for yourself."

"But you can tell me about my relationship with Gregory and you, but you refuse to tell me about my parents?"

"Kelsey, I have only provided you with information about your relationship with Gregory before you married him and from a best friend's perspective. I don't believe it's my place to do so regarding your mother."

"Why not? You've supposedly known me since I was a teen. Who better to give me a glimpse of how I interacted with my mother?"

"Hasn't your mother given you enough information? Are you doing the exercises with her, with the photo albums, and trinkets?"

"I've looked over those photo albums a thousand times, and searched every inch of the house, and still not one photo of my father."

"Why do you think your mom doesn't have any photos of your father?"

"If I could answer that, I would probably figure out what my mother has been hiding possibly for years."

"Why do you think she's hiding something from you?"

"You haven't been listening again. You're telling me the love of your life dies, and you would not keep some kind of memento?"

"I never said it wasn't odd, Kelsey, and I can't answer why your mother acts the way she does. I can tell you that she's always loved you."

"Loved me? In the twenty-something years you've known me, you can honestly say that I had a very strong and loving mother-daughter relationship with that woman?"

"I'm saying that your mother loved you no matter what."

"But you didn't answer my question."

"Sure, I did, Kelsey. Times up. I'll see you the same time next week, right?"

I can't explain how horrified I was when I got the call that my only child had been in a serious car accident. Every single last inch of me was filled with terror at the thought of losing my little girl. I don't even remember driving to the hospital, nor breathing, for that matter. I just kept praying over and over, "Lord, let my child live! Please let my child live!" And He did. Thank you, Lord. Seeing her lying in that hospital bed, bruised and all bandaged up made me cry so hard that I had a headache for three days.

I have to admit, Kelsey and I have had a rough relationship over the years. All in all, I still love my baby and raised her the best way I knew how. With kids nowadays, loving them as much as I do Kelsey isn't always enough. These days your children want to be your best friend; want you to be the parent when they need something and nonjudgmental all at the same time. Call me old fashion, but in my day, children were respectful to their parents, no matter how old they were. Not today. My daughter has yelled, screamed, and even cursed at me, all in the namesake of personal freedom. That has always been Kelsey. Don't get me wrong, I didn't raise her to be disrespectful and I don't think she means to be, but she has entirely forgotten all she has been taught: "The fear of God and the fear of the rod will raise a good child."

I blame all of those stupid magazines, talk shows, and movies that have brainwashed Kelsey's generation into believing that life should be lived by the seat of your pants. I call it the "instant oatmeal generation." With the use of technology and all that is accessible to them, younger generations are used to receiving anything and everything in an instant. Press a button, and your dinner is cooked; push a few more buttons, and any information you desire appears on a computer screen. Gone are the days when to cook a bowl of oatmeal; boiled water in a pot; waited for the water to percolate; poured in the oats; stirred while they cooked; and then waited five more minutes for the oatmeal to cool down so that you could eat them without burning yourself. Everything is at their fingertips or is within reach. Most of them switch jobs every two paychecks trying to race up the ladder and stepping on everybody along the way.

That was Kelsey. Extremely ambitious, determined, and ready to knock over anything that would hinder her dreams. It was almost poetic to see how my frail little girl could grow to build a small empire in a blink of an eye. Becoming so successful so quickly has turned Kelsey against me. I believe she loathes having me for a mother because I'm not as successful or as ambitious as she would have hoped. I could see it in her eyes even as a child that she would quietly pass judgment on me with every decision I made. Whether right or wrong, those cold glares often made me feel as if I were the child, making me second-guess my own choices. If the choice were positive I thought maybe I could have done it better and if my instincts were wrong, those unforgiving eyes would pierce right through me. I don't see how anyone can live up to Kelsey's high expectations. They should name a street after Gregory for all that he has endured with her. Still, she continues to push everyone she knows, and we are not permitted to let her down. We are all supposed to behave like trained seals; on our best behavior so that she appears to have a perfect life.

It's a shame that I love this child as much as I do. I call her my child because that is what she will be to me until I'm gone. I know she's a beautiful grown woman, married with children, and a successful businesswoman, but to me, she'll always be my baby. The day Jamie discovered that she might have amnesia was so confusing. There I was, staring into Kelsey's face, and she didn't even recognize me. She didn't even recognize herself, for that matter. She kept looking into a mirror across from her thinking that there was someone else in the room with her. She was talking to her own husband the father of her children as if he were a stranger. I worked at a nursing home for most of my life but, had never seen anyone so young suffer from memory loss. I can't imagine having every memory, every experience, and every hurtful thing that I had undergone erased from my mind forever. I couldn't wrap my mind around losing all of the time that I spent on God's green earth. It was like having the opportunity to start over—having the opportunity to be reborn as an adult—having the opportunity to renew relationships with my family, my husband, and my children.

Somewhere deep within me, when Jamie introduced me to my daughter and she looked at me in disgust, I saw an opportunity to redeem the time that I had spent, wasted, or lost, with her. I saw the perfect opportunity to rebuild a solid foundation for a mother-daughter relationship that did not exist between us. I saw an opportunity for me to also have amnesia from our past and make a fresh start. Was God giving me a chance to redo the last 30-something years, turn back the hands of time and allow me to have a loving relationship with my baby? I could see this opportunity like the writing on the wall, but I would first have to make sure that Gregory and Jamie would not interfere with my good fortune.

On the night that Jamie called a family meeting to discuss Kelsey's current condition and homecoming, I had a headache all day long. As Jamie and the others milled around talking and comforting one and other, I knew I had to make sure that whatever Jamie suggested, would not impede me from being able to restore or start a new relationship with my baby. I had to make sure that no one would give Kelsey a full glimpse of our distressed past. I knew that my intentions were good, but I couldn't be concerned whether people understood why I had to do what I knew must be done. I needed a little redemption. It was no one's business, and people shouldn't judge me on the mistakes I made in the past, and how they've affected Kelsey. What mattered now is that I have the opportunity to move forward with a healthy attitude and develop a strong relationship with my only child.

"Let's see, I think that is it for right now." Jamie concluded after giving us a quick overview of how we are to deal with someone with amnesia.

"Jamie, if we are to assist Kelsey in gaining her memory of us and her life, how much information should we give her?" I asked at the ready.

"Good point, Mom. Listen very carefully. In cases like Kelsey's, it is very important that we give her as much information about her life as possible."

That was not the answer I was hoping for. How can I delicately get her to say what I want without making people suspicious or giving away my plan?

"Does that mean that anyone can tell Kelsey what they think my relationship with her is like? I don't think that's right, Jamie. I want Kelsey to get to know me, not what another person thinks my relationship is with her. I mean, wouldn't that be considered gossip?" Gregory chimed in. I've always loved my son-in-law.

Jamie replied, "You've got a point, Gregory. The best way for Kelsey to rediscover all of us is through her current experiences with us as individuals in hopes that that will jumpstart her memory. Okay everybody, let's make a pact that we will only speak of our own experiences with Kelsey. This way we can ensure that we don't sway Kelsey one way or the other. Agreed? Mom will only make mention of Kelsey's childhood, Gregory will talk only about the children and their marriage, and I will fill in the blanks about her school and years as a single woman. Debbie, as her business partner, you will fill her in regarding her career and client relationships at the firm. The rest of you will only discuss the personal experiences that you shared with Kelsey. Agreed?"

"Agreed. What if she asks us about other people or stuff she thinks we might know about?" Debbie Martin asked.

"Blame it on me. Let her know that as her therapist I suggested that you interact with her in this manner," Jamie responded.

"Who could know Kelsey better than her own mother? You mean if she asks me something I cannot answer based on my perspective?" I asked baiting Jamie. Since Jamie will be spending the most time with Kelsey in therapy, and she has known Kelsey the longest and witnessed many years of my relationship with Kelsey, this was my way of throwing off any suspicion of my intentions.

"Mom, though you have known Kelsey the longest it may be best if we are all as neutral as Switzerland if Kelsey tries to discuss relationships with other people." Jamie finished hoping that would curb urges to add my two cents about anything when talking to Kelsey. "We must be respectful and allow other people to have a fair shot at rebuilding their relationship with Kelsey. Agreed?"

"Agreed," we all said in unison. I could not have asked for a more perfect scenario. Gregory was content in knowing that this was his opportunity to stand up and be the man Kelsey deserved.

However, there was an uneasy feeling in the pit of Jamie's stomach. Professionally, she wasn't sure that what she just suggested would be the smartest thing. However, she was hoping that some unresolved issues that plagued Kelsey all of her life would finally be resolved so that her best friend would be able to move forward. It was time for Kelsey to stop carrying around the pain from her childhood. It was time for her best friend to release the stress that strained her marriage to Gregory and start living a completely fulfilled life. As her best friend, Jamie vowed to herself that she would assist Kelsey in any way she could to help her obtain peace.

Chapter Six

Gregory

As I lay in bed watching Kelsey sleep, I gaze at the angelic face of the woman who hates me. I know hate is a strong word, but what else can I conclude from the way she has treated me since the accident. It's hard to believe that after five years of marriage, Kelsey has no recognition of me whatsoever. She looked so peaceful lying next to me with her left hand tucked under her pillow. Her hair is wild around her face, and I can't help brushing the soft strands from in front of her in order to get a better view. Her long lashes look as if they are waving hello to me, and her beautiful full lips make her simply irresistible. She's so lovely that I can't help myself; I leaned over and planted a soft kiss on her forehead. As always, truly I adore her.

On the day of Kelsey's accident, strange things were happening all day long. First, I left the house to go to work only to find that one of my tires was slashed. Then, I get to the office, and everything seemed to go wrong: one client cancelled an important meeting, and another never showed up due to a scheduling mix-up. My boss's face said it all; he thought I was a total screw-up. Not to mention, my cell phone was ringing constantly throughout the day but when I would answer it, they kept hanging up on me. Lastly, I come home to find my nanny packing my children's clothing and notifying me that, per my wife's instructions, she was to take the kids to an undisclosed location.

"Like HELL you are!" I shouted. "Hold up. I need to speak to my wife first. So just sit down until I find out what is going on."

I had to fire the woman who had raised my kids for over five years just to stop her from taking my babies out of my house. Everything seemed to be falling apart that day, and by the time Jamie called to tell me Kels was in an accident, I was almost suicidal. As I rushed over to the hospital, tears were streaming down my face. I could not imagine losing Kelsey. I could not picture living without the woman I instantly fell in love with so many years ago.

I can remember it like it was yesterday. A few friends invited me over to the local bar for a few drinks during happy hour. In walks this tall, long-legged, dark-haired beauty, and I almost fell off of my barstool. My friend Johnny was saying something to me, but all I could hear was the boisterous laughter of an amazing-looking woman from across the bar.

"Forget about her," Johnny commented. "Mike tried to talk to her weeks ago and she was cold-blooded. Besides. her friends are like bulldogs. You'll never get them away from her long enough to talk to her."

"Well, then I will have to talk to all of them," I stated as I stood up to approach the group of women who were already rolling with laughter.

"Why do you wanna walk into a pack of hyenas? Say one word and they'll all fall out laughing, Bro," he added tipsily, but I was determined. "You are a brave man, Pritchard."

When he put it like that, I had to admit I knew I was setting myself up to catch a brick, but I didn't care, and I had to meet her. So, I walked over not trying to be cool or anything, looked the beauty in the eyes, and said, "Hello." She smiled coolly, nudged one of her friends, and as they all turned around, she held up her left hand to reveal a large wedding ring on her finger. My bad. I threw my hands up as if to say sorry and turned around to retreat back to my seat. I can't speak for all men but whenever I get shot down it always feels as if I retreat in slow motion. As I went back to the bar and took my seat next to my friend Johnny, I squint my eyes shut and shook my head. I always seemed to pick the married ones.

"Don't sweat it. You never want to get to know someone at happy hour."

"Excuse me?" I said turning to my left looking directly into the eyes of a tanned-skin beauty holding a glass of champagne.

"Was that a rhetorical question or did you really not hear me?" she replied exposing a sinister smile with white teeth. She, like the other woman, had long dark hair but she had a heart-shaped face with full lips. I couldn't speak because her huge doe-like eyes were piercing as if to look right through me, and I didn't want to sound like a jerk. So, Johnny jumped in.

"He's a good-looking guy and not as slow as he may seem."

"I'm sorry you caught me off guard with your comment." It was the sanest thing I could think of to say without looking like an idiot.

"Oh, I apologize. I should have given you a few moments to pick your face up off the floor before I said anything to you." Feisty. Me likey.

"I'm Gregory Pritchard."

"Nice to meet you, Mr. Pritchard. I'm Kelsey Smith."

"Now that my face is off of the floor, can I get you a drink?"

"No, thank you, I limit myself to one champagne glass of ginger ale during happy hour. I've gotta head back to the office." With that, she turned and walked over to the group of ladies and took her seat right next to the long-legged woman I wanted to meet, and all of her friends started laughing. I'd been played. They must have seen me looking at their friend and sent Kelsey over to the bar as bait when her friend kicked me to the curb.

"What just happened?" Johnny questioned.

"I don't know, but I'm in love," I responded.

"Man, she's a black widow spider, can't you tell?" "I know my type and she's it."

"Bro, you're toast, and a glutton for punishment!"

Maybe, but I liked her, so instead of trying to act cool by playing as if I was uninterested, I made my move.

"Kelsey, it was nice to meet you. I've decided to take your advice and would like to invite you to my friend's art gallery Saturday. Though you didn't get a chance to formally meet him, my friend Johnny Kittson owns an art gallery on South Orange Avenue called *Sixty-One*."

"I know that place," one of her friends stated. "It's cute and showcases some of the most prolific artists and art pieces."

Kelsey nodded as if to approve. "Isn't that the place where we went a couple of months ago to see Arthur Laurel's work?"

"That's the place," I continued.

"Well, Mr. Pritchard, thanks for the invitation. Who will they be showing on Saturday?"

"There will be a collection of artists from the Caribbean. I hear it's very colorful and lively. The food and drink theme of the night will reflect the art presentation."

"Hmmm…I've been looking for something to go in my new office space. Again, thanks for the invitation." She was playing it cool, and so would I.

"You are more than welcome, and I hope you and your friends will stop by. Ladies…"

As I turned to walk back, I could feel them already beginning to whisper about me, and their eyes were already burning a hole in my head.

"What happened?" Johnny asked in disbelief. "I've never seen anyone talk to that group more than three seconds.

"I invited them to your gallery."

"Smooth, Bro. Very smooth."

"What good is it for me to hang around you if you aren't gonna be useful? Women like art and I even invited the friends, too."

"I'm really impressed. You have officially become my hero."

I was a wreck on Saturday. I couldn't get Kelsey Smith out of my mind, and since I had no way of contacting her, all I could do was wait to see if she would show up. I would have been devastated if she didn't show, but she did. Thank God she came with only one friend. I was not up to entertaining the entire pack tonight.

Kelsey came gliding into the gallery as Johnny was about to toast the artists in the room. She looked very elegant in her navy-blue strapless dress and matching heels. Her long chestnut brown hair was swept back with a matching navy band and soft tendrils that fell across the face. A simple invisible chain hung with a princess cut diamond floating above her cleavage. She was stunning, and her bronze tan set the perfect backdrop for the stone. Her friend was just as attractive with her long dark hair, naturally tanned skin, and hazel eyes, and looked to be of Mediterranean descent. She was dressed in a beige pants suit, and her olive skin made her look classic and wealthy. These weren't the type of women I was accustomed to dating. They were both too well put together.

"Mr. Pritchard, nice to see you again. Thank you for inviting me to the gallery. I am a huge art fanatic."

"You are more than welcome, and I am glad to see that both of you were able to make it."

"This is my friend, Dr. Jamie Hyman."

"Hello," Jamie said as she quickly walked over to a painting. "Can I get you a drink, Kelsey, or should I say, Mrs. Smith?"

"You can say either Miss Smith or Kelsey." We both laughed aloud.

"Whew. Glad to see that I didn't try to pick up another man's woman." She smiled.

We talked all night, and I even took her to Café Domino down the street for dessert after the gallery closed. We must have talked for hours over that one piece of cheesecake. It was amazing. Kelsey was witty, beautiful, and had a great sense of humor; she was not shy by any means. We have been inseparable ever since. The day I made Kelsey my wife in front of 300 guests was the happiest day of my life. So much so that while at the reception and jamming to some Caribbean music, I spontaneously did a cartwheel. Kelsey always joked with me that whenever she got mad at me she would just remember *the cartwheel*.

When I arrived at the hospital, it was chaos. Doctors and nurses were running around, and Mom was wailing like a madwoman, "My baby, not my baby." Jamie was a big help informing us of her status, and she took care of all of the paperwork. Jamie was my savior. My job was to try to keep my mother-in-law calm while holding it together for myself. I never felt so helpless. There was nothing I could do but wait outside of the emergency room while they tried to put my wife back together. I had never been so scared in my life. But when Jamie informed me that Kelsey was in a coma after seven hours of waiting, I lost it. I broke down right in front of everybody and I didn't care that my muscular frame was doubled over and crying like a baby. I didn't care that I started praying, begging God to heal my wife and bring her back to me. I didn't care how it looked or that my nose was running. I just wanted my wife back in my arms again.

Jamie had to give me a strong sedative to calm me down so I could take a nap in the waiting area. When I woke up a few hours later, it all felt like a dream until I saw the emergency room sign in the waiting area. Jamie was slumped in a chair next to me, and Mom was wide-awake, talking to herself and staring into space.

"You okay, son?"

"For now. Any word on Kels' condition?" "Nothing as of yet."

"Oh no! I forgot to call Joanna and tell her what's going on!"

"I took care of it and spoke to my grandbabies. She's gonna stay with them until you get home, so not to worry."

"Thanks, Mom."

"Gregory, I need to have a serious talk with you. I don't know how long our faith will be tested and how long Kelsey will be out of it, but I want you to not give up hope. You just continue believing that everything is gonna be alright. You hear?"

49

"Yes," I replied weakly as the possibility of Kelsey out of my life came into full picture. I had always relied on Kelsey's strength for everything. She was a fantastic mother and organizer. I'll never know how she was able to manage a household, run a successful business, take care of the kids, juggle her clients and friends, and still save time for me. Thinking about how wonderful she has been all of these years only made me feel more selfish and intimidated about my shortcomings. I knew I was a hard worker, but everything just seemed to turn to gold for Kelsey without any effort. I kind of felt less than the man she needed me to be.

"Gregory!" Mom shouted.

"Yeah," I responded turning my attention back towards the conversation with my mother-in-law.

"I need you to pay attention right now. Those babies need you to pay attention, and so does Kelsey. You are gonna have to step in and pick up the slack for those boys. Once they find out what happened to their mother, they're gonna need you more than ever."

"I know, Mom, I don't know if I can do this," I whined.

"Would you like some cheese with that 'whine?'" she asked and we both fell out into roaring laughter. That was one of Kelsey's favorite lines she would use on the kids to get them to stop acting like a baby.

"Seriously, I'll be there to help you, but you are gonna have to lead your family like never before. I know how hard it must be to have to contend with Kelsey's strong personality. But you are gonna have to be strong for my daughter right now."

"The problem isn't Kelsey's personality; it was that I never had to want for nothing when it came to the household. Kelsey was just Kelsey. I never had to manage the checkbook, drop the kids off or deal with Joanna. I went to work, went out with the boys from time to time, and spent time with my wife," I admitted.

"Well, I know you've had it pretty good, but those days are officially over. Life begins. Kelsey has always been a take-charge woman, and she does it so well that it seems effortless. But that is no excuse for your not helping out all of these years. You are gonna have to make some sacrifices until Kelsey is back on her feet. I hate to say it, but she spoiled you too much; still, that's no excuse. You're going to have to give up your friends for a while, and your weekly basketball games. "

She was right. I was able to live a carefree life all of these years because Kelsey took care of everything.

Jamie woke up and went to check on Kels. When she came back, we were able to go in and see her. Tears began welling up in my eyes. She looked like a wreck. I couldn't remember a time that my wife looked so helpless. So many tubes were coming out of her body, and she was hooked up to numerous machines. Lord God, please help her. We stayed in the room with her for a couple of hours, then Mom suggested that I go home and be with the boys. Though I didn't want to go, I knew she was right. Our sons were four and six at the time of Kelsey's accident, and I knew that they probably could sense something was wrong. They were extremely bright for their ages. Before I left, I asked if I could be alone with Kelsey for a moment. As everyone left the room, I fell to my knees and held my wife's limp hand. I began to speak.

"I don't know if you really know how much I love you, Kelsey, how much I have always loved you. Since the moment you zinged me in the bar, you had my heart, and you still do. I know that I have not always been as supportive of you and that I have an extremely immature and selfish side. I don't know if it's because you made everything easy for me, or if it's because I've been trying to hold on to my childish ways. But I promise you right now, Kelsey, those days are gone. It's time for me to stand up and be the husband you desire and will need. Someone who is committed to you and our sons, 100 percent. Lord God, please hear my prayer. You know my heart. Know that if you bring my wife back to me, I will do everything I need to do for my family to get through this period so that we can live a full and happy life. I ask this knowing that I must pay my vow. Have mercy and bring my wife out of this."

I got up feeling 10 lbs. lighter and determined to start my life anew for my family. I kissed Kelsey on the lips and walked out of her hospital room needing a hug from my boys. As I drove away from the hospital, I noticed that I had messages on my cell phone. I checked my voicemail and discovered I had ten voice messages, all hang-ups. Time to grow up, Pritchard. Dude, it's time to grow up.

As the memories filled my brain, tears began flooding my eyes. I lay in bed looking and admiring a woman who doesn't even remember who I am, anything about our marriage, how much I love her or appreciate all I have done since her accident, and it hurts. It hurts mostly because she can't remember my face, my heart, or our memories. She looks at me in pure disgust, and nothing I do can please her. Still, I made a vow, and I will honor it. How easy it would be if she could just remember *the cartwheel*.

Chapter Seven

My Grandfather

I cannot tell you how obsessed I had become with trying to figure out who I am and where I came from. Since my mom has been so evasive about the "father" subject, I started asking about my grandparents and extended family members. I would sit and stare at the images that she would present to me; boxes or trash bags full of old photos delving into them for hours at a time. I wouldn't eat and rarely went to the bathroom on those visits with my mom, who, by the way, was insistent upon not letting the photos leave her house.

Staring at all of the faces, some of which resembled mine and others so strikingly beautiful, was fascinating. Looking through all of the old photos sometimes made me feel alienated. I did have a chance to interact with some of my cousins and extended family members on my mother's side at a couple of family gatherings. Watching them stare at me with plastic smiles, trying to figure out what to say next amused me. It became a game I would play trying to see if I could innocently rattle them with my condition. I know that sounds cruel, but it was true. I would accidentally say jarring things to see if I could get a rise out of them. I would compliment them on how nice they looked, then I would slide in a quick, "For your size you look great," or "Were you always this big?" It was so fun to see how either my mom or Gregory would dance around my comments trying desperately to clean them up. I know it wasn't right, but how else is someone who had no clue of half of the people around her going to entertain herself?

I would also try to get answers out of them about me or my father, and of course, my mom, or Ms. Kerri-Claire, as I liked to secretly call her, would always ease herself into the conversation rattling off obscure facts. Whenever possible, I would try to corner my mom's cousin, Pauline, who was very close to my mother and people thought I favored, to grill her for facts about my father. She was always so kind and gentle with me but never gave me any scoop.

"Do you know much my dad loved me?" I would probe.

"Baby, I know that you were loved by everyone you came in contact with," she'd answer and smile.

"Were my parent's very much in love?"

"That's your mother's story to tell. It has been suggested that the only way to really help you in your condition is not to bombard you with too much too soon. Now, if you want to know about how much you have always been my favorite cousin, then we'd be here all day. I would rather focus on you remembering how much I love you than talk about things that can't be changed." She was so gentle that she almost made me forget how she totally evaded my question.

"Well, can you at least tell me why no one on your family's side talks to my father's family? Does anybody know where they are and how I can get in touch with them?"

"Precious child, sometimes it's best to know one-sided love than two-sided confusion."

What the heck does that mean? Foiled again! I swear they're all in cahoots.

Both of my mom's parents were dead but they made a beautiful couple. The pictures of my grandmother Virginia, or Jamie as they most often called her, were of a petite but stylish woman. She had a lovely round face, long dark hair, and wide eyes that almost seemed too big for her fragile face. Her beauty was regal, and she seemed safe in the arms of the man she loved. She died when my mom was a teenager, so my mom, like I, grew up an only child.

The one thing I do know is that my mother's father was the patriarch of the Rollins clan. Though he was the youngest of eight siblings, his large frame and broad features demanded respect from his older siblings. His name was James Christopher Rollins, and I loved him. How do I know this? I cannot say for sure, but I just know that I must have and still do. The way he stands tall in his pictures, commanding attention, and respect. My mom says I have his domineering attitude, but there's no way I could have ever been such a well put together person as he appeared to be. His salt and pepper wavy hair, dark colored almond-shaped eyes, and smooth brown skin made him look debonair in his fashionable tailored suits. He wore his favorite hat, a gray tweed fedora, pulled down low over his forehead and cocked to one side. I'm told his friends used to say he looked like "old money" even when he wore his postal worker uniform. To me, when he wore his hat, he looked more like a journalist on the search for the next front-page story than a civil servant. I've been recently watching old movies on cable, and I would say that my grandfather had the style of Humphrey Bogart, the stature of Jimmy Stewart mixed with the glamour of Clark Gable. Well, that's what I like to think.

I've never heard one unkind thing spoken about my grandfather from anybody, often speaking of him with great admiration. His piercing stare seemed to go right through you, and everyone on his block, including the adults, saw my grandfather as a father figure. He was said to be kind and loving, stern, and respectful. In a word, he was a gentleman. He was a man who was fortunate enough to have been raised by strong loving parents, and not victimized by life's circumstances, like my mother and me.

I could tell that he loved me too based on all of the pictures he took with me when I was a child. Other than my mother, I was the only other child my grandfather held as an infant. Maybe it's because I was his only grandchild, but I like to think it was because we had a strong bond for each other. I wish he were still alive. I've been told that he spoiled me rotten. Always lavishing me with gifts and praises, and that this strong male-figure would run around acting like a big child whenever I was present. There's even a photo of the two of us having tea with two of my dolls; he had arrived for the tea party dressed to the nines. There's a picture of us playing together in a huge pile of leaves when I was about five or six years old, and I can almost hear the crunch of the leaves under our feet. I wish I could remember him and this moment.

From the very first photo I saw of my grandfather, looking at him has become the closest sense of home that I've ever had. His image is my shelter and brings my restless soul to a peaceful state. To me, he is the definition of what a dad or husband should be like—the perfect symbol of manhood—strong, proud, protective, and gentle. That's what I see when I watch the old movies of him with our family. My grandfather treated me like his own child, with loving affection—he protected me.

My favorite home movie is of the two of us playing on the front lawn. I must have been about seven in this clip. He kept teasing me, "KeKe, what's this?" pointing to my forehead over and over until I answered him. "KeKe," that's what he called me in the home movie. It must have been his pet name for me, and I'd fall for it every time by asking, "What's what granddaddy?" He'd smile exposing his pearly-white dentures while pointing to my forehead.

"This looks like a good place for a Stick-Up," he'd state falling into roaring laughter.

"Mom, what's a Stick-Up?" I asked walking into my mother's kitchen.

"A what?"

"A Stick-Up. Granddaddy referred to it in the home movie I was just watching, and I don't understand why he was laughing so hard."

"That's because he got you. Dad used to like to play that joke on people."

"But I still don't understand it."

"A Stick Up was an air freshener that that was sold in the '70s.

Dad loved to play practical jokes on people, so he would divert your attention onto something and "get you" by repeating the tagline from the commercial. I guess you had to be there, but my father would fall out laughing if he were able to pull off the joke. He'd get us almost every time. He was a sly one," she explained.

"I see. So, this was our private little joke," I fantasized.

"No. Your grandfather used to do that to everyone including the people in his church where he was a deacon."

It sounded so corny, but I loved it. The fact that my grandfather, the perfect portrait of manhood, could let down his guard and be silly in his old age was just darling to me. If he were around today, I know I would not feel the sense of loss or longing I have for my real father. At least I have some evidence of our relationship and I plan to cherish his photos and home movies forever.

Chapter Eight

Meeting My Mentor

The day I met my Mentor was one I will never forget. Several months after my accident, and after begging my mother for weeks, my mother finally took me to the church where my grandfather served as a deacon for 13 years. Our family, kids, and all drove out together one sunny spring morning to the church that my mother attended as a child. It was set on the opposite side of town in a small middle-class community. I could see its large brick structure with huge glass doors halfway down the block. People were milling around outside of the church greeting each other with holy hugs and handshakes. I felt like a little kid in my seat and sprang out of the car once we parked. Gregory followed close behind grabbing the hands of our kids and trying to keep up with my fast pace.

"Slow down, Kelsey. Let's walk in as a family," he whined.

As I reached the northeast corner of the intersection, trying to wait patiently for the others to catch up, my mom began to complain. "Why are you in such a hurry? You're gonna give me a heart attack walking that fast!"

"You'll be fine. Hurry up, I want to get a good seat," I said motioning them to get a move on.

"We'll be fine, Kelsey. You don't need to rush, there is enough room for everybody," Gregory added.

Except I already knew there wasn't. As we walked through the front doors, I could smell the flowers from the altar all the way in the back. Fresh lilies garnished the purple, gold, and red altar. Huge windows were on both sides of the sanctuary, there were chocolate-colored pews, and dark wood beamed ceilings were high above us. Even though the sanctuary's seating was in a semi-circle, you could clearly see from where we were standing that there were no seats left. I shot Gregory and my mother a quick look as the usher tried to sit us in the back of the assembly and Gregory quickly spoke up.

"Is there a section for first time visitors?"

"First time visitors you say?" The old gentleman looked as if he were sucking on a piece of candy and repeated himself as if he weren't expecting us to answer him.

"No, we don't have a 'First Time Visitors Section.' We're not one of those TV evangelists but we do get a pretty good crowd of people in here each week. Where are you visiting from?"

"We are the family of James C. Rollins. He used to be a deacon here many years ago. This is his daughter, Kerri-Claire Smith, and I'm his granddaughter, Kelsey," I chimed in, hoping that my response would get us a better seat.

"You're Deacon Rollins' peoples?"

"Yes, we are. I'm his daughter," Mom answered proudly.

"Let me see what I can do. Wait right here. Now don't move or I can't help ya out." He walked off lickety-split.

"Kelsey thinks she's at Club Jesus." Gregory leaned in teasing me as we sat down, and my mom laughed.

Say whatever you like, but I got my way. We were seated in the 7th row. After service, my mom bumped into some old acquaintances, and I sat in the pew for a few moments taking everything in. I could just picture my grandfather sitting on the dais or helping with one of the ministry teams, and I wondered why he never became an elder since he was so well-liked. I wondered what this place looked like when he was alive. It was obvious that it had been remodeled since then. As I was walking up the aisle with my children, I heard a man ask if I was Deacon Rollins' granddaughter. I replied, "Yes, I am. My name is Kelsey. Did you know my grandfather?"

"I sure did. He was a wonderful man," the kind elderly gentleman replied.

"How did you know my grandfather?"

"We were very close. I was a good friend of his when he and his wife lived on Merkel Avenue. I knew him for many years; until the day he died."

As my kids ran to their father, I became intrigued with this man. Did he know about my father? Who he was and what happened to him? Could he tell me more about my grandfather and my childhood?

"I remember. I knew you when you were just a little girl about this high." BINGO!

"Well tell me then, was I as cute as they say?" I smiled. He chuckled.

Ever since that day, my Mentor and I have been the best of friends. I've always thought of him as a Mentor because he has a way of giving me an alternative way of looking at things. He has a way of pulling out the best of me. My Mentor's warm and gentle demeanor, his soft but strong voice was laced with love and insight. He was the only older gentleman I had to rely on as a father figure since every other male figure was either dead or lived too far away to build a bond with.

At first, we just began casually speaking over the phone, but a phone call here and there quickly became lengthy talks for hours at a time. I thought Gregory would be jealous of all the time that I spent with the elderly man, but he actually encouraged it. He said our conversations always seemed to put me in a pleasant mood. That's probably because I longed for a father figure and my Mentor gave me fatherly wisdom. Gregory didn't have much of a choice, but I guess it was good that he felt as if he did.

"So, tell me, what did you do for a living?" I questioned him in one of our late-night conversations. I wanted to know everything about him.

"I was in construction. Wanting to build things was instinctive to me. I would simply see something in my mind, say what I wanted to build, and poof, it was done," he replied.

"That's neat. Did you ever build anything with my granddaddy?"

"Though James looked handy, his talents were best served in other areas." We laughed.

"That bad, huh?" I asked still laughing.

"No, not that bad, but he left the building stuff to me. He was a great helper though. I used to teach woodshop classes, and he was always there to help people with their projects."

"I bet you did a lot of work on the church."

"Yep, I've always loved building places of worship and worked on many in my day."

I sighed and could imagine this kind old soul hammering away at a plank of wood with my grandfather handing him tools or nails or something corny like that.

"Why don't you tell me a little bit about your husband, dear?"

"Well, there's not much to tell. I'm married to a guy that I don't remember anything about, and I don't even know how to get to know him," I answered honestly.

"Have you tried talking to him?"

"That's all he ever wants to do. He's a talkaholic! I don't think Gregory and I have that much in common. He doesn't seem like my type. I mean, he's obviously handsome, but there's no chemistry between us."

"Is there chemistry on Gregory's part?"

"Well, yeah. He tells me all of the time how much he loves me and how beautiful he thinks I am, but, well, I don't know."

"What don't you know, child?"

"I don't really care how he feels."

"Why do you say that?"

"I know it must sound crazy or extremely cold, but I don't feel a thing for him. I feel closer to the pictures of my grandfather than the man with who I made two beautiful little boys."

"So, are you saying that you are more in love with a family member in a photograph than your own husband? What about your kids? Do you love them more than your husband?"

"What I'm saying is that it is easier for me to feel something towards the kids, even though I have no idea how to handle them or their sticky little fingers, but that's another story altogether."

"Kelsey, I'm concerned. You are married to the man, not the kids. You should be focusing on working on your relationship with Gregory first and foremost," he advised and was probably right. But, oh well.

Chapter Nine

The Babysitter

Imagine for a moment that you are lying in a hospital bed with a throbbing headache, a stiff back, and a dry mouth. You've been up half the night in pain, and you can't sleep comfortably on your stomach. Then imagine faintly hearing soft voices chanting, "Mommy! Mommy!" As I parted my lashes to get a peek without letting too much daylight in, I saw two little round faces staring back at me, my mom standing behind them, and they were all giggling.

"Don't say that about your mother!" my mom snickered.

"Well, she does! Doesn't she, Jesse?" the smallest one said. The tallest one giggled loudly.

"Yep, she sure does."

These are my kids. Dr. Jamie and told me that I was the mother of two little boys—Tommy just turned four and Jesse was six years old. They had the cutest little faces with huge eyes, and the youngest one looked exactly like my mom. The oldest one leaned over me chewing and chomping on his gum in my face. I could smell the sweet scent of sugar on his breath as I pretended to be asleep.

"Can she hear us?" Jesse asked as his juicy spit hit my face.

"Is she dead?" asked the pint-size one.

"Stop saying that! She's just asleep," my mom corrected him.

"Oh. I still think she looks like a mummy."

They all laughed. A mummy! I'll fix them. Playing along, I started groaning and moving my stiff arms like a real mummy.

"Urrr..." I groaned loudly.

"AAAAAAHHH!" They squealed and ran behind my mom.

"Who are these little rug rats?" I asked opening both eyes slowly.

"MOMMY!!!" They both squealed in unison and raced towards the bed almost knocking over the machines connected to my arms.

"What happened to you Mom?" "Does it hurt, Mommy?"

"Jesse hit me in the car!"

"No, I didn't! It was an accident!"

"Nuh-uh!"

"I did nuffing."

"You're always teasing me!" Tommy whined.

"AM NOT!"

"ARE TO!"

Welcome to my world.

With all of their noise, I'll never know how in the world I could not remember their loud mouths. It was like that on every visit. One would pick on the other, then the other would tell, and then the little one would start screaming as if the older one caused him undue pain. What the heck was I thinking having these two little munchkins? Oh, and it didn't get any better once I got home. To see them in full form was scary. The little one was always trying to sneak sugary sweets; he gets hyped up on the sugar, and then runs around like a dinosaur. I'm not kidding. The both of them hunch their backs, curl, and tuck their arms close to their chest and jump out at you when you least expect it, roaring like a T-Rex. The first time they jumped out at me, I almost had a heart attack. They came from behind doors, leaping out at you with their wide mouths open and then scamper off before you could get a chance to swat at them.

I have to admit it; they are two of the cutest little things I have ever seen. Now if they only made muzzles for little boys, we'd be in business. I have scanned over their baby pictures trying to recall any moment of their lives and I feel so inadequate. If it weren't for the scar

Tommy left on my belly from the C-section, my slim figure yielded no proof that I ever had kids. I can't imagine what it must be like for them to wake up one day with their mother in the hospital and her not able to remember them. I tried everything I could to not let on that I had no clue who they were or what they were talking about half the time. I always tried to make them as comfortable as possible around me, but to tell you the truth, they bugged the hell out of me. Thank God for our nanny Joanna. She's been my saving grace with the kids. Lord knows I feel like I'm the babysitter when she's around. She's got raising them down to a science. She understands their every need, and they naturally respond to her.

"It sounds like you're a little jealous of Joanna," my Mentor suggested.

"Does it really? I don't think so. I'm so grateful for her help that I don't think I have time to be jealous."

"Kelsey, you do realize that even though you have great help, you are still their mother, and have to form a bond with them. Boys need their mother's love."

"I guess so, but they are still young, so I have some time to work on that. Right now, I want to focus on getting used to their sticky little hands touching everything."

"Do you know that Tommy's favorite color is red, and that Jesse loves green?" he questioned.

"I never really thought about it. That might explain why Jesse is always in that raggedy old green hat," I laughed.

"A mother automatically knows these things, dear. Don't you want to?"

"So, are you saying that I'm a bad mother because I don't know their favorite color?"

"What I'm asking is, don't you want to know? Now is the time to create memories with the boys by spending time with them and getting to know them. How else do you think it will happen?"

"I didn't think about it that way."

"It's too late to think about it; you must begin now before they believe that Joanna loves them more than their own mother." He had a point.

The next day I planned a full day of activities for just the boys and me. We went to their favorite diner for breakfast, spent the day in the park racing boats, and it was a blast. I even got a chance to see them in their own world playing with other kids their age at the playground. The little one won't admit it, but I think he ate a bug.

"No, I didn't."

"Yes, you did."

"NO, I DIDN'T!"

"YES, YOU DID!"

"Gentlemen, that's enough! Tommy let it go." "Mommy, I'm Jesse."

"Oops, sorry about that, you two look so much alike."

"Hey, you don't even know our names!" Tommy surmised.

"I know your names—you're T-rex and you're Raptor." "Cool!" they squealed in unison.

The truth was, I did have a hard time remembering who and I was think this just bought myself some time. We were having a ball laughing and telling funny stories, and it was so much fun hanging out with them. I didn't feel pressured to be anyone other than who I was at that moment. No pressure to remember.

However, things changed when we got home. I was preparing a late afternoon snack for the kids when the phone rang. It was Dr. Jamie. After pulling off their dirty clothes and helping them wash their hands, I began to fix PB&J sandwiches to hold them over until dinner. Instinctively, they began to run around the kitchen making so much noise, I couldn't hear myself talk.

"Gentlemen, can you keep it down or go into another room? Mom is on the phone—anyway, I think I made some real progress with the boys today," I continued my phone conversation. As I began preparing their snack, I popped open a new jar of grape jelly and began to spread a healthy helping of the sweet goop onto a wheat bread slice. I could hear Jesse's voice in the background trying to politely get my attention. I briefly looked up, but I ignored the little guy, and I kept spreading the jelly on the bread as I was talking to Dr. Jamie.

"Mommy?"

"Jesse, can't you see Mommy is on the phone right now?"

"But Mommy—"

"Not now, Jesse!" I shouted growing impatient. As I turned, I could see his eyes filling up with water. What now? I mashed the second piece of bread with a sloppy helping of peanut butter on top of the jelly-soaked piece and slid it over to him as I juggled the phone cradled under my chin. Tommy had already started eating and was already asking for cookies with half of his sandwich still in his mouth. On the other hand, Jesse just stared down at his sandwich as if it were a foreign object.

"Jesse, eat your snack." I said I said in a strong tone thinking that he wanted some attention because I blew him off for my phone call moments before. He didn't budge. His little face began to pout, and I could swear he was staring at me as if he wanted to kill me.

"Jesse, dear, I am losing my patience. You asked for a sandwich, and I made it for you, so eat it. There are too many kids in the world who go hungry every day, but you have food, so be thankful and eat up. Mommy will be off the phone in a second. So, Dr. Jamie, what do you think is the problem?" I asked returning to my conversation. The next thing I knew, this little militant midget jumped out of his chair and threw the sandwich across the table yelling at the top of his lung with tears streaming down his face.

"I WISH MY OLD MOMMY WAS HERE RIGHT NOW!"

"WHAT! JESSE I *AM* YOUR MOTHER AND DON'T YOU DARE SPEAK TO ME IN THAT TONE!" I shouted back.

"Kelsey, calm down. Yelling won't solve anything. Ask the child what is bothering him," Dr. Jamie offered. Always a therapist I guess. Jesse was crying so loudly that I could barely hear what else she was saying. I calmed down and questioned him.

"Jesse, why would you say such a horrible thing to me?"

"You don't know me!" he cried. I tried to reply that I did know who he was. He was my firstborn son Jesse who I love very much. I tried to comfort him by putting my arms around him, but he broke free and ran off shouting and the top of his lungs.

"NO, YOU DON'T! MY REAL MOM KNOWS THAT I DON'T LIKE JELLY! I WANT TO GO STAY WITH MY GRANDMA!" he belted out as he raced up the stairs. No, he didn't!

"Oh yeah, well you just go ahead and stay with Ms. Kerri-Claire. Try screaming at her like that and see what happens. She'll make you go outside and pick your own switch so fast your head will spin. Then she'll tear your bottom up so you won't be able to sit for a week. GO 'HEAD, LIVE WITH HER; SEE IF I CARE!" I finished loud enough so he could hear me all the way upstairs.

"Can you believe that kid?" I asked, returning to my phone call with Dr. Jamie. Then it hit me. "Oh, my goodness, Dr. Jamie, I just remembered something!" I squealed like my four-year-old. Jumping up and down, I started doing a little happy dance. I forgot that I wasn't alone and turned to see my wide-eyed, four-year-old looking back at me as if I were crazy.

"Mommy remembered something. Isn't that great?" I joyfully explained.

"Good job, Mommy. Can I have a cookie?"

Chapter Ten

Bad Dreams

"Can you believe it? I remembered something!" I proudly told my Mentor later that evening. I continued "and Gregory said he was proud of me."

"That's great, Kelsey."

"What's wrong?" He didn't sound as happy as I expected him to.

"Everything is fine, it's just…well, don't you think you spend a lot of time being concerned about the past?"

"In my condition, I don't think I have a choice."

"Why do you say that?"

"Right now, there are so many unanswered questions that have to be answered in order for me to move forward. I want to know more, or anything, about my dad, and what my mom is hiding. I want to know more about my relationship with my husband, and I want to know the meaning of these stupid dreams I keep having." Was that too much to ask?

"Baby girl, you keep trying to dredge up something you no longer have control over. Sometimes you just have to release stuff and trust that the answers will come on the wind."

After our conversation, I was more confused than ever. My Mentor had made his point, but it was the first time he had mentioned that I needed to release things I couldn't control. That's like telling a dog not to be a dog, a shark not to be a shark, or a control freak that there's nothing to control. It was just plain unnatural.

The next day I went to see Dr. Jamie. She was so proud of me, and we did a few new exercises to see if I could regain any additional memories, but nothing happened.

"Don't be worried, Kelsey. Sometimes it takes a couple of jumpstarts to get the brain to start working properly again," Dr. Jamie said.

"I know, but it's hard not to be disappointed."

"Look, Kelsey, Rome wasn't built in a day, and even though it's been almost a year, this is a positive sign. Something is trying to get out, and we are just going to have to take baby steps to get through it." She seemed very upbeat as I recanted my conversation with my Mentor.

"Kelsey, when was the last time you had one of your dreams?"

"Last night like every night."

"Tell me about it."

"Well, there's not much to tell except I was lost in the woods again."

"The same woods?" she asked.

"Yep. The very same woods. Why do you ask?"

"It's just that having reoccurring dreams about the same location leads me to professionally believe that they may represent the current state in your life."

"What do you mean?"

"Well, it is likely that the woods represent your household or…"

I cut her off.

"What about my marriage? Or the relationship with my mother?"

"Yes, it appears that the dreams are symbolic of the current stage of your life and/or they may represent one of the scenarios you just suggested."

"Is it possible that they represent all of the scenarios I mentioned?"

"I suppose, but that would be a very aggressive assessment. I mean extremely aggressive. Are you having the same dream, or does it vary?"

"It varies but not like I'm dressed differently. One night I'll be in a completely different area of the woods, and sometimes I'll recognize a boulder or tree trunk. Is that weird?"

"Why don't you tell me about the dream you had last night so that I can get a better understanding of how to decipher it?"

I took a deep breath, closed my eyes, and began to describe the horrible night I had. I wouldn't consider my dreams nightmares, but they can be troubling. I've tried to talk to Gregory about them, but he always has little interest in them. I think he's the cause of them.

Last night, I woke up into a dream in unfamiliar territory. I was still cold and hungry like all the other times before, but this time I felt as if I knew where I was going. As if I almost knew the way out. I could faintly hear cars up ahead, and I got so excited that I began to run towards the direction of their sounds. As I began to pick up speed, I tripped over a dead tree trunk, and I landed flat on my face into a huge pile of wet fallen leaves. As I lifted my head, I could feel them stuck to my face and in my hair. It felt like something was crawling on my face, and so I sat up quickly, slapping myself vigorously trying to get whatever it was off of me. It was a snail.

"Yuck!" I shouted.

I got up and feverishly brushed myself off. My hair was stuck to my back and hung limply from the light rain that began falling. I began rubbing my hands together trying to keep myself as warm as possible as I continued to walk towards the road. I could hear the sounds of the cars getting louder. My heart started to beat a little faster with excitement. As I broke out in a slow jog, the rain began to fall harder. Its drops make a rhythmic thud on the leaves that were already lying on the woodland floor. My breath became heavier, forming a visible train of cold air coming from my parted lips.

I guess I became overly excited because I twisted my right foot on a slippery rock and lost my balance again. However, this time I didn't fall headfirst into leaves, but I was lying eye to eye with a dead dog whose snout was literally two inches from my face. Bugs crawled out of its mouth, and its lifeless eyes were looking straight at me even though they had partially rolled back into its head. The combination of wet dog hair and death gave off a strong stench. I jumped up quickly backing away from the poor thing and walked carefully around it. By the time I focused on the road up ahead, it was getting dark. I knew that my survival depended on moving forward. As I walked, I could still hear the buzzing of the flies that were hovering over the poor pooch's body. The image of the dog's face was stuck in my mind even though several minutes had passed. Questions about the dog started to flood my head. What was a dog doing out in the middle of the woods by itself? Why would someone leave it there? Was it a stray, or did it have an owner? I became so preoccupied with the stupid dead dog that I eventually realized that I had veered off course, and it was too dark to remember the way I came. I can't get a break. It seems whenever I get close enough to escape this wooded hellhole, it draws me deeper into its core.

Dr. Jamie looked at me with a blank stare when I finished recanting the dream. She was so quiet, that for a second, I thought she might have drifted off into a daydream.

"Dr. Jamie?"

"Sorry, Kelsey. I was processing what you just said. I have a question for you. Do you remember what kind of dog it was?"

"It was hard to tell the exact breed; it looked like a mutt, and it was covered with sticks, leaves, and lots of dirt."

"Did it look like it was buried?"

"No, not quite…just dirty and dead. Why?"

"I think the dog represents the things in your life that are currently dead."

"What dead things?"

"Your past and all the things you can't change about your current situation."

"I don't think so. I mean, it was just a stupid dog."

"Was it?"

"Yes. Things live, and things die. That's the circle of life. Everything has an expiration date."

"Interesting. If the dog was so stupid or insignificant, why was its image so ingrained in your mind?"

"I don't know why. Maybe I was shocked at the sight. I wasn't expecting to fall and come face to face with someone's dead pet."

"I mean, you were concentrating on the dog so much that it caused you to lose sight of the freedom you knew was just up ahead. Isn't that strange?"

"What's strange is that you think the dog represents something in my life. Okay, Dr. Jamie, riddle me this. What does the dead dog represent?" I decided to turn the tables on her for a little while.

She took a deep breath, stood up and walked over to the small office refrigerator in the left corner of her office. As she pulled out a bottle of water, she coolly said, "I am certain that the dead dog is your lost memory. You have the capability of moving forward, but you keep getting distracted by unanswered questions of your past." I was quiet so she continued to take a sip of water.

"I also believe that your dream, or all your dreams, are trying to tell you that even the slightest distraction of your past will cause you to miss out on current opportunities if you keep focusing on insignificant things."

"So, you're telling me I shouldn't dream? That's hooey, Dr. Jamie. I don't consider trying to remember how I got to become the woman that I am, or was, as an "insignificant thing." I am moving forward. I spent all day yesterday trying to connect with my kids, and I've been faithful in coming to our sessions. My searching for answers is also a big part of looking to move forward…"

"Once your questions have been answered?" she interrupted.

"Well…yes. As you just said, Rome wasn't built in a day."

"Touché."

"Next week I will be turning two years old, and I believe I have made significant progress. Wouldn't you agree?" She opened her mouth to speak but hesitated.

"I guess that depends on what your goals were for this year."

"What does that mean?"

"If your goal was to barely remember anything, just recently try to connect with your children, and not connect with your spouse at all, well then…you seem to be right on target."

Chapter Eleven

Two Years Old

"Are you assuming that I am stalling or not putting forth any effort to get better?" I asked. I was insulted and she was beginning to piss me off.

"Don't get mad, Kelsey, but look at where you are. Where did you want to be at the end of this year, and have you accomplished all that you set out to obtain?"

"Hmmmm…shouldn't that have been something that my *"therapist"* could have helped me identify when we started these sessions?" I asked, giving her much attitude.

"Maybe, but this is *your* healing time. If you don't have an idea of where you are going, how will you know once you get there?"

I didn't say much after that; I was too pissed to continue. If I understood her correctly, *I* should have had some sort of master plan in order to gain my memory back. My only problem with that scenario is that I believe that should have been her job to suggest it in the first place—she's the professional. She's the one getting paid from my insurance company. I was so mad that I excused myself and went to the bathroom to calm down. As I sat in the stall, my mind started racing. What kind of doctor was she anyway? Furthermore, don't get me started on how much of a friend she has not been from the onset. What gives her the right to harangue me with that crap? I tried to calm down, but nothing helped. The only thing I could think of was to call my Mentor. I took out my phone and wildly punched in his number. As I began recanting my conversation with Dr. Jamie, her assistant knocked on the locked bathroom door to see how I was doing.

"Mrs. Smith-Pritchard are you okay in there?" she asked.

"Yeah, I think so," I answered. "I know that I have lost my memory, but I do still remember how to pee!"

"Okay, well let me know if you need anything."

"Toilet paper: check. Seat liners: check. Nope, I seem to have everything I need!" I answered sharply.

"Kelsey, that wasn't very nice," my Mentor scolded.

"I know, but I'm in the bathroom! A place of privacy, and she was being bothersome," I whined.

"Now, Kelsey, do you want some cheese with that whine?"

After hanging up with my Mentor, I slunk back into Dr. Jamie's office.

"Are you okay?" Jamie asked concerned.

"I'm fine."

"Are you sure? You've been in the bathroom for over an hour and a half."

"Sorry for holding you up. I know that you have other patients to see," I said truly apologetic.

"Don't mention it. I was able to see another patient while you were in there."

"Well, I'm going home to think about what you said today and see if I can come up with an answer to your question."

"Kelsey, I hope you aren't offended. My questions were to make you see that whatever your answer would have been, it doesn't matter. Looking back isn't going to give you the answer. I think the main objective now should be to identify what you want to obtain by the end of your second birthday. Understand?"

I woke up Saturday morning to the off-key singing of Tommy and Jesse's rendition of *Happy Birthday*. Their little voices cracked each note as if they were hacking through a piece of thick wood. It was the sweetest thing I had ever heard.

"Happy Birthday, Mommy! I made this picture for you yesterday in class," exclaimed Jesse with pride. "It's a picture of you and me holding hands and walking to the store to buy your birthday gift, but I only have $4.16."

"Honey, what did we buy?" I asked looking intently at the detail of the picture he had made me. With his keen eye for detail, he so eloquently drew me with a heart-shaped face, huge eyes, and long brown hair.

"ICE CREAM!"

"Mommy, I got you something, too!" Tommy announced not wanting to be left out.

"Really, what is it?" I asked holding my hand out and closing my eyes tightly.

"No Mommy, it's a hug and a song," hitting my hand out of the way. He gave me a long hug and then began to sing loudly.

"Happy Birthday to you! Now that you are two, I'm still older than you!"

"Is that so? Then why am I taller than you?" I asked tickling them both feverishly.

"Cause you are the Mommy T-Rex!" Jesse managed to choke out between his high-pitched laughs.

"And don't you ever forget it! The Mother T-Rex is the strongest and fiercest dinosaur in the land." I let out a loud roar, and they began to chime in with their little vicious howls. We must have made a huge ruckus because, the next thing I knew, Gregory entered the room looking at us as if we had all lost our minds. We continued to roar and growl for a moment, but Gregory's stern stare made us all feel a little silly, so we finally calmed down until we had completely stopped. As he turned to leave the room, he quickly snapped back around and jumped on the bed with us letting out his poppa dinosaur snarl. It must have been a sight to see all of us jumping on the bed letting out prehistoric yells. I have to admit, it was the most fun I can remember having with my family to date.

"So, what do you have planned for today?" Gregory asked.

"Not much. I sure don't want to go through last year's fiasco," I answered carelessly.

"What do you mean? I thought you liked your party last year," he sounded hurt. I had forgotten that he had planned the whole thing.

"It was okay. It's just that it was a bit much, don't you think? It was the first time I had been surrounded by so many people at once, and it was very overwhelming."

"Should I cancel tonight's party then?" he asked sarcastically.

"Would you? That's if you've planned another family get-together."

"You want me to?"

"Please, I can't take another night like that. I never know what to say or how to answer everyone's dumb questions."

"Kelsey, you are so ungrateful. I went through a lot of trouble to plan that party, coordinating people's travel arrangements from out of town. All of the arrangements were a hassle and, not to mention, your mother drove me crazy with all of her questions. WE HAD OVER 350 FAMILY AND FRIENDS IN THE HOUSE!"

"Why are you shouting at me? You should be thankful that I don't want to put you through all of that this year," I responded. What an ingrate.

"Kels, it's too late. Everything is already done."

"Well just cancel it. Save yourself the trouble." The phone rang. Saved by the bell. As I answered it, Gregory looked at me in sheer shock. He started pacing back and forth, then stopped, stood with his hands on his hips, and started shaking his head and talking to himself before walking out of the room.

"Hey, Mom. Thank you. Yes, I feel great."

"I'm so proud of you. You just keep on believing, baby, and everything will be alright. You're gonna get your memory back in no time," she said cheerfully.

"Thanks again. Mom, could you help me? Gregory has planned some big party for tonight, and well…I don't want it."

"What do you mean you don't want it?" she yelled into the phone in high dramatics. "We have all gone through a lot to plan this party, and it would be selfish of you to make us cancel it after all of our hard work."

"Mom, please don't make me go through with it. I swear I'll have another memory lapse if I have to bear such a taxing night like last year."

"Well, why didn't you say so before? Did Gregory know you didn't have a good time last year?"

"It seems nobody did! Look, I don't know what the big deal is. It's my birthday, and I don't want a stupid party. Just cancel it, okay? I'm sorry for snapping, but you guys are acting like a bunch of babies." With that, I slammed down the phone.

As I stepped into the shower, the phone rang again, but I didn't answer it. It was my birthday, and I didn't want to argue. It was a moot point; I didn't want to have a stupid party. I was not gonna back down and suffer through another one of my family get-togethers. Had they forgotten that my husband's cousin Michael, who after a couple of drinks, got into a fistfight with his wife right in front of all the kids? Or that someone spilled red wine on my good rug in the living room? Not to mention, I was accosted all night long by all of those strange people. No way am I going through that mess again. Those people are fortunate that I even let them come to my house for holidays after all of that mess. Matter of fact, to this day, we still don't know who cracked the glass tabletop on the dining room table. I had to special order a new tabletop to replace the broken one, and it cost me over $6,000 to do so.

I guess you could call us wealthy. We lived in a sprawling six-bedroom, five-bathroom home in Chatham, NJ, which is a very affluent suburban neighborhood a few miles away from my successful law firm in Short Hills. Even though I was fairly young to open my own firm, Dr. Jamie told me that one client I assisted in a class action lawsuit brought about a 14 million dollar payday. As his attorney, that meant a third of the awarded monies went to my firm for my legal services. That payday afforded us our luxury home—paid in full—with all the fixings. That case brought attention to the firm from other clients, and Smith Pritchard & Associates has become very successful in less than three years.

The first time I stepped into my house, my own jaw dropped. With its high ceilings and marbled entry way, the 5200 sq. ft home looked larger than it felt. Filled with a mix of high-end contemporary and traditional furnishings our red brick center hall colonial is as comfortable as any home. Its large rooms give us the ability to not be on top of each other, which was a big help during my recovery. It took me the longest time to figure out how the kids, who not only have their own rooms and a huge playroom on top of the garage, can still manage to leave their toys all over the house. No home training!

We have a gourmet kitchen that looks out into our large backyard. We even have every imaginable upgrade that you could have put on a house. It's a good life. I stepped out of the shower to answer the ringing phone and almost slipped on the cold brown Italian marble floor.

"Hello." It was my Mentor.

"Hey, birthday girl. How's it going so far?" he asked.

"It's a nightmare," I answered dramatically. I've been hanging around Ms. Kerri-Claire way too long.

"What's wrong? Who's upsetting you on your big day?" His tone was extremely protective.

"Everyone. They want to throw me another unbearable birthday party tonight."

"I know. What's wrong with that, Kelsey?"

"Et Tu?"

"Why don't you want your loved ones to do something nice for you today?"

"You make me sound horrible. I just don't need people making such a big fuss. It's bad enough that we aren't celebrating my real birthday. I feel like an idiot."

"Why?"

"Well, because it's my fault that I'm in this predicament in the first place."

"No, it isn't."

"How about hanging with a bunch of folks that I can barely remember their names is little embarrassing," I confessed.

"Why don't you tell that to Gregory? Is he so unreasonable that he won't understand?"

"I don't know. You should have heard him yelling at me a minute ago. I guess I can understand why though. He went through all of the trouble to make the preparations for a celebration tonight and all."

"Give the man some credit, Kelsey. Just talk with him and be as honest as you can without being rude."

"Do you really think I'm rude?"

"You can be rough around the edges, but inside you have a heart of gold."

I felt like a heathen by the time I got off the phone with him. Was I that insensitive to everyone? Tears started to well up in my eyes, and as I silently released them, I could hear Gregory entering our bedroom. I quickly ran the water and splashed a healthy dose on my face to conceal my tears.

"Kels, if you don't want the party, I'll cancel it."

"It's not that I don't want a party, honey, it's just that having all those people around me only makes me feel even more inadequate," I confessed as my Mentor suggested.

"Baby, I don't want you to feel as if you've done something wrong. We just wanted to show you how much we care, love and are supporting you," he said sweetly as he held me in his arms.

"Would you mind if I plan something just for the two of us tonight?" Where did that come from?

"What do you mean?"

"Let us do something together for a change. No kids, or my mom; just the two of us." Out of all of my symptoms, I never knew it also included Tourette's syndrome.

"Really, just the two of us? You mean it, Kelsey?" he asked pulling me close to him.

"Yes. I'll arrange everything so don't worry. What time to do you want to escape?"

"I'll leave that up to you. In the meantime, I have to start calling all of our folks to let them know that the party is cancelled," he shouted back as he left the room whistling. I can't believe I just suggested a date for the two of us.

Since my homecoming, Gregory and I haven't spent a lot of time alone. Though he had suggested it on several occasions, with all that has happened to me, I wanted to take things slow regarding our marital relationship. It's not easy to wake up one day and realize that you're married to a man you don't remember only to have him look at you as if he expects you to perform your wifely duties. I don't think so. Even though I watched our wedding tape and read the love letters we had written to each other, I still don't feel anything for him. He's really sweet, and there are moments that I can tell he is trying his hardest to be tender but, I'm sorry, there was still no connection.

On several occasions, I had grilled Dr. Jamie about my old love life after finding several photos and mementos from past boyfriends. She would never give me too much detail on them other than obvious answers. For the most part, they were all career-driven like me, and usually much older. She did mention that she liked Gregory the best because of his tender heart. He wasn't a game player, and from what she knew, he had never lied to me once. He was a good man who dedicated himself to me from the moment we met.

"Before I met Gregory, did I mention that I was frustrated with my love life?" I asked Dr. Jamie during one of our sessions last month.

"No. Why do you ask that question?" she replied.

"Just wondering. Can you tell me anything about the men I dated?"

"Like what?"

"You know, did I have a particular type of guy that I was attracted to?"

"Kelsey, you never had a certain type. You liked all kinds of men and they liked you."

"Okay…let's try this again. Was there a commonality in the men I was attracted to? For instance, did I prefer green eyes to brown? Muscular? Tall and thin or short and stubby? Blue collar? White collar? Come on, give me the scoop," I playfully pleaded trying to get her to let down her guard.

"Let's just say you were an equal opportunity employer." We busted out laughing in unison.

"What does that mean?" I asked still chuckling.

"Well, your type has always been good looking men," still giggling she blurted out, "Preferably white."

"What?" I questioned shocked at her admission.

"Look, Kelsey, you were attracted to those that were attracted to you, and you have a lot of male colleagues who were white. There has always been an air about you that makes men comfortable, and that can be extremely attractive to all kinds of men, and you gravitated towards successful, extremely handsome, and exotic older white men."

"Then how in the world did I end up with Gregory?" "What's wrong with Gregory?"

"Well, to hear you tell it, I liked good-looking, rich older men. How did I end up with someone not as accomplished as I, and a few years younger than me?"

"Are you saying that you don't think Gregory is good-looking and successful?"

"No, that's not what I'm saying. It's just, I know that Gregory is having trouble at work closing deals and landing new clients. He's just very different from what you just described. Never mind, I was just curious and making conversation," I lied, and I never lie.

"Kelsey, maybe he's been having a tough time because of all that has happened in the last two years."

"I know—I know I have considered that possibility."

"Let me make it plain for you; Gregory swept you off your feet."

We had been living like roommates for the past two years. Though Gregory has been a big help with the household, kids, and taking care of me, there was a side to him that made me think he was kind of corny. Kissing him was like kissing my arm. I remember a couple of months ago we were laughing about something, and he leaned in quickly giving me a sloppy wet smooch. I tried not to pull away too quickly, and when he started making these moaning sounds as if he were Casanova, I almost busted out with roaring laughter. He began pawing my hair and briefly got his wedding ring caught in my long locks. I just sat there with both eyes open looking at him, and when I had enough, I politely unglued myself from his clutches. I know that must sound so cold for a wife to say about her husband, but it was the truth. As clumsy as he was, it's a wonder he fathered two kids. Maybe I can jumpstart some memories if I connect with my husband, so maybe this dating thing isn't such a bad idea.

I planned an early evening picnic at a local park complete with a gourmet picnic basket. It's funny, but I have been so disconnected from Gregory that I had no idea what kinds of things would make me amorous. So, I figured I'd start with food. You can't go wrong with a roasted herb chicken with all the fixings. We laid a blanket down on the grass and talked as we ate our food. It was a warm summer night, and the crickets entertained us with their song. After dinner we took a paddleboat ride, which we almost turned over because Gregory kept teasing me saying he wanted to see me soaking wet. I yelped for mercy as he would sway the boat trying to tip it over—we had a ball. However, the best part of the evening was playing in the playground. Gregory snuck a kiss in as he was about to push me on the swing. I have to admit, it wasn't as bad as the last kiss, but I still felt nothing. As we walked into the house from our date, I noticed an oversized floral arrangement in the foyer. It was the ugliest thing I had ever seen. Stuffed in a plaid multi-colored basket it had all sorts of long weeds, baby's breath, and carnations. *Yuck!* Who died?

"Why did Joanna leave this in the entry way?"

"Don't you like it?" Gregory asked.

"Should I? It's summer. Why is she leaving Easter bonnet-themed floral arrangements around the house?"

"Kels, those are for you?"

"What, are you expecting to attend my funeral tomorrow?"

"What?"

"You bought those for me?"

"Yes, for your birthday."

"Why would you order me anything with carnations in it?"

"I like carnations."

"You would." He was silent.

"Gregory, you don't give carnations to a woman. They are not a gesture of love. Take a memo; I like roses."

"I can't believe you."

"What's to believe? I had better arrangements sent to me while I was in the hospital. Did I like carnations before my episode?"

"Yes, you liked all kinds of flowers; it was never such a big deal."

"Well, note to self, carnations are for funerals, holiday table arrangements, or what you can give to a temp at the office for National Assistant's Day. They are not the appropriate flower to send to your wife. Especially when you're trying to get lucky! Got it?"

"Kelsey, you sure know how to ruin a good day. Goodnight."

"I ruined it? I didn't send myself a bunch of ugly weeds," I called out as he walked up the stairs.

Chapter Twelve

Homecoming

The next morning, Gregory and I didn't mention the argument we had the night before. It was forgotten. We laughed, joked, and watched movies with the kids enjoying a lazy Sunday at home. It was very relaxing. Gregory must have snuck out when I dozed off mid- afternoon because I don't remember him leaving to get the beautiful two dozen peach and white roses that replaced the monstrosity of a floral arrangement that contaminated my foyer last night. Like I said, all's forgiven. I even gave him a quick kiss to say, "thank you." To repay my kindness, he presented me with a beautifully wrapped box.

"For me?"

"Yes. I wanted to give it to you last night but, well you know."

"Thank you."

"Open it, Kels," he said, seeming more excited than I was.

"What is it?" shaking the box.

"You'll see if you open it."

I ripped the pretty paper off the gift and opened the box to find a gorgeous crystal heart-shaped box.

"Thank you, it's wonderful."

"Are you sure you like it? I can always get you another one."

"It's perfect," I said as I pecked him on the cheek.

"I thought you would like to add it to your collection."

"What collection?" I didn't remember seeing a collection of anything this pretty in my house.

"In your office."

"What office?"

"Your law office in Short Hills, silly."

"Oh, right, that office."

"What's wrong?"

"Nothing, I guess. It's just that I don't remember my office at all."

"Well, I was hoping you would visit it soon. Maybe even go back to work."

"What's wrong, are we broke or something?" I asked, panicked.

"Don't be ridiculous. I just thought since you've mentioned that you get bored sometimes that you might like to check up on your firm and its clients."

I hadn't really thought about it. For the last two years, I was so focused on regaining my memory that I hadn't even considered going back to work.

"I think that is a great idea. Kelsey, there is nothing you love better than to work," my mom said when I told her about the box and Gregory's comments on the way over to my office. "Besides, everyone misses you," she added.

"How do you know?"

"I speak with Debbie, your associate partner, often. She's another hard-working woman. I don't see how you two do it; run a business, manage a household, and juggle the kid's schedules."

"Mom, that's what the hired help is for."

"That was mean."

"I don't mean it to be. I meant that you get the right help to assist you and things run like a well-oiled machine."

My office was less than four miles away from my home and it shared the 5th floor with another law firm that specialized in international law. As I walked out of the elevator, I found myself really nervous. As a matter of fact, I was petrified. I had no idea what

I was doing there and why in the heck did I bring my mother with me? As scared as I was, seeing the facial reactions of my receptionist when I walked through the door was priceless.

"Mrs. Smith-Pritchard, welcome back! It's good to see you," the receptionist said as she quickly hung up the phone. It must have been a personal call.

"Thank you," I would have said her name had I remembered it.

"Do you want me to announce your arrival?"

"No need. I want to surprise everyone just like I surprised you." I cunningly smiled at the well-dressed two-something woman. She offered a fake half-smile realizing that I must have known that she was running up the office phone bill. Standing in front of the dark marble entryway and looking at the company nameplate in large gold letters, *Smith Pritchard & Associates,* on the wall was thrilling.

"Was I obsessed with the color brown?" I asked my mother.

"What are you talking about, Kelsey?"

"I mean, was there a sale or something?"

"I still do not understand your question, dear?'

"This reception area and my bathroom have the same Italian brown marble." She laughed loudly.

"I never thought about it before, but I guess they are. Maybe it was one of your phases."

"I think it looks nice. Rich and regal," offered the receptionist as she promptly answered a call.

"I like it, too, Kelsey. It's powerful. It's not what you would expect from a law firm owned by a woman, that's for sure. That's what you always wanted."

"What do you mean?"

"Your career has always been very serious to you. I remember the first internship you took while you were still in law school. Do you know you cut your waist length hair to your shoulders because you didn't want it to be distracting? Personally, I thought you were out of your mind. It was as if you were sabotaging your looks so that people would take you seriously."

"Did I really do that?"

"Yes, you did."

"I was an idiot."

"No, just extremely ambitious. There's nothing wrong with that. Your hard work paid off."

"How long did it take me to grow my hair?"

"Many years."

"Like I said, I was an idiot."

Walking through frosted glass double doors exposed a staff of twelve who were equally shocked to see me as well. You'd think I had returned from the dead. Mom got stuck talking to several people outside of Debbie Martin's office as I entered to say, "hi." Debbie was the only person I had seen a few times since my accident. "What a wonderful surprise!" Debbie said as I sauntered into her large office. "What brings you here?"

"I just came to check out the place. How are you?"

"Fine. Well, a little disappointed that you decided to cancel your birthday party."

"I wasn't up for it. I'm still trying to recover from the one last year."

"So, are you ready to get back to work? I could use your expertise." It sounded sincere but I would have sworn she was fishing. I didn't have a chance to honestly respond since my mom burst into the room.

"Debbie, that's a cute suit!"

"Thanks, Kerri-Claire. How have you been?" They kissed their hellos and chatted.

Debbie had a large office with a wall of glass windows. She had decorated it with dried flowers and warm colors of jade green, beige, burgundy, and rust. It reminded me of a postcard of Central Park that was stashed in one of Mom's bags of photos. I don't see how she could get any work done in such a comfortable space. It looked like someone from one of those home-decorating shows got a hold of it. I quietly walked past Debbie and my mom as they ran their mouths talking mostly about nothing. I turned to my right and walked past the conference room, which was behind a wall of glass. Adjacent to the conference room was a locked door that led to my office. One of the paralegals rushed to open it for me, and I politely nodded my head and said thank you.

As I opened the door, the bright sunlight from outside momentarily blinded me. As my eyes adjusted to the brightness, I could see the lush office lavishly designed in beige with accents of gold, deep purple, and dark green. Walking towards my desk, I passed the overstuffed leather beige sectional, which wrapped around half of the room, and a wall of glass windows ran the entire length of the room from ceiling to floor. Unlike Debbie's office, my space was regal. I pulled out my new crystal box and placed it on a beige-marble wall unit that was behind my beige marble desk, which was lined with crystal picture frames of my family and more colored and crystal boxes. I turned to face my desk and noticed that on the wall directly across from it hung a huge antique gold mirror above one side of the sectional. My hands instinctively ran across the front of the dark green leather executive chair that was fit for royalty. *Welcome home, Kelsey.* There was a presence of power, of wealth, of respect, and it felt good.

"There you are. I thought you went to the bathroom. What do you think of your office? Pretty nice, uh?" my mom probed.

"It's definitely me," I confidently replied.

Chapter Thirteen

My Mentor & Granddaddy

On the drive home, I fantasized about my office. I could see myself sitting at the elegant marble desk strategizing with clients or working the phones. I saw myself sitting at the head of the caramel-colored marble conference room table delegating tasks to my staff. It was the first time that I saw a glimpse of the woman I used to be that wasn't a Kodak moment. Funny, even though I live in an affluent neighborhood, I didn't feel wealthy until I walked into my office. I felt as if I had arrived, a force to be reckoned with, instead of the powerless amnesia victim I had been for the past two years. I liked the way my staff looked at me, and the respect my presence commanded. The elegance of my office also explained why I had all of the expensive designer suits that filled my walk-in closet. The feeling was very seductive.

So much so that I was not able to concentrate on the one-sided conversation I was having with my mother. She seemed quite happy entertaining herself with the sound of her own voice, so I just let her ramble on. I didn't mean to be rude, but I was too preoccupied with the thought of the huge windows in my office and how calming its scenic view was.

When I was back in my office, and while my mother was speaking with one of my assistants, Vera Win, I had discovered a secret door that led to a private green marble bathroom with a shower stall. My professional world seemed fascinating, and I wanted to know more about whom I was and how I could mentally abandon all of it.

—◦◦◦—

"I used to be a big deal!" I declared to my Mentor.

"Why do you say, 'used to be?' You still are in my book," he sweetly stated.

"You know what I mean. I hadn't realized that I was so important. I mean, my clients counted on my legal intellect. You don't understand what that feels like."

"What do you mean?"

"I've had to rely on so many people to exist during this period of my life, and it has always made me feel uncomfortable. This ordeal is like being born again after relying on others to look after me."

"You make it sound as if you had to relearn everything." There was a hint of sarcasm in his voice.

"Well, I did have to learn about all of the people in my life, and that seems like everything to me. So, I know how to ride a bike or cook a meal, but not being able to remember loved ones or people who work for you can make you feel a little kooky. Walking into that office today made me want to be that person again."

"Who were you?" he questioned.

"I can't answer that question just yet, but I like being portrayed as a businesswoman, not just Gregory's wife or mother to my kids."

"Why, because you were successful and influential? I wonder what people who worked for you really thought of you."

"You make it sound as if I did something wrong."

"What did you do right?"

"I obviously had to bust my hump to get to where I am."

"Did it ever occur to you that maybe you were at the right place at the right time?"

"You mean my whole career was just a coincidence?"

"No, more like a blessing. Sometimes people receive a gift and do nothing to earn it, but don't mind taking credit when credit is not always due."

"That's harsh. You mean I should not be excited about what I have accomplished even if I can't remember the steps it took to get there?" I didn't like where this conversation was going.

"I think you should be able to recognize that what was accomplished might not have had anything to do with you, but more likely a blessing from above."

"Well, maybe I could have easily recognized it as a blessing if I didn't have a law degree and all of my awards as proof of my abilities," I boldly stated.

"Baby girl, you have a lot to learn."

"Well, I'm tired and this conversation is boring me. I'll talk to you tomorrow." I was pissed and wanted out of this conversation.

"Sweet dreams," he concluded.

I was so heated after my phone call with my Mentor that I tossed and turned half the night. I couldn't believe our conversation. I simply called to tell him how excited I was about possibly returning to my practice, and he made me sound as if I was an ogre. To make matters worse, I'm back in the stupid woods feeling hopeless. I'm sitting on a tree stump with my head cradled in my hands as my arms are resting on my knees almost about to cry. Confused, frustrated, and lonely, I can sense that I'm not alone. As I lift my head to peer at the sky, birds linger above. I can smell the faint hint of death, and the stench gets stronger as the wind blows from the northeast. It's the gross smell of the dead dog. Why me? My tears begin to fall freely as I look down to see some creepy thing crawling on my shoe. I'm so tired and pissed that I don't even bother to shake it off. I give up.

What's the use in trying to move forward if everyone constantly makes you feel as if you are gonna mess things up? What's the use in trying if people are gonna continually beat you over the head with what you used to be like? Maybe I was a tyrant. What's wrong with commanding a little respect from those who I gave a paycheck? What's wrong with that? Am I supposed to just go through life making sure everyone else's existence was carefree and easy while I am forced to work hard to make sure other families are fed? It didn't seem fair. I'm so tired of feeling like I'm responsible for every Tom, Dick, and Harry who didn't get enough hugs as a child or who has tissue paper feelings.

"I refuse to carry that burden!" I shrieked loudly." I've got my own kids' lives to mess up." I was blubbering freely but could hear the sounds of leaves crunching under footsteps. I quickly turned and was startled to see my grandfather standing several feet away from me. I was so shocked that my mouth hung open widely at his presence.

"That's a good place for a Stick Up!" he said pointing to my dropped jaw.

"Are you really there, Granddaddy?" I asked in disbelief.

"Yep, a Stick Up!" he laughed.

I ran and hugged him tightly, but he just stood there with the same half-smile on his face. I felt as if I were hugging a hologram image of him, but I didn't care. I just cried, and he just stood there letting me. When I was able to gain my composure, I let go and stepped back to get a full glimpse of him. His expression never changed, but when he spoke, it was as clear as a digital recording.

"Don't worry, KeKe. It's time to grow up."

"What do you mean? I'm grown, Granddaddy?" I answered.

"No, you're not; you're only two years-old," he replied.

"Have you seen my kids? What's heaven like?" I asked.

"Heaven starts in here," he said as he motioned to my heart. "Just keep walking and one day you'll get out. It took me many years, but you'll get out sooner."

What the heck does that mean?

"Granddaddy, I want to go home right now."

"You can't; you don't even know what home looks like. I gotta go now KeKe. I love you," he said turning around and walked deeper into the woods.

"Granddaddy don't leave yet. I need more time with you. I need to remember you, please don't go!" I pleaded hysterically as I followed him but collapsed into tears onto the ground. The more I wept, the further and quicker he walked until he was gone. I was distraught. I was laying in the fetal position holding my head, crying profusely. So much so, that I woke up with a tear-soaked pillow.

Gregory woke up and tried to console me by hugging me, but I was a mess. I told him about the dream and begged him to give me answers as to why I kept having them.

"Baby, I don't know."

"Is that all you can say?" I asked as I tore out of his embrace.

"Kelsey, you are upset, come here. I don't know how to fix it, but I want you to know that I am here for you."

"Then tell me why the men in my life always abandon me?"

"What are you talking about, Kels?"

"First my dad, then my grandfather. They both left me." "I'm here, Kels, and I'm not going anywhere."

I didn't say it, but I wanted to scream at the top of my lungs— *FOR NOW!*

"Don't even get me started on Debbie Martin. She's probably having a ball running what I built. I'm surprised she hasn't moved into my office."

"Why do you think that Kelsey? She's been a saint taking on your clients and running the business so that you and your family can continue to live the lifestyle you have become accustomed to. She deserves a raise and full partnership," Dr. Jamie offered.

"You weren't there. I know what I felt. I need to see the books. Then I can tell you if she's doing a great job or not."

"It's understandable that you would want to make sure everything is running well. Let me ask you a question; if you are so concerned, why don't you just go back to work?"

"I'm not ready yet."

"You sound ready." I had told Dr. Jamie about my trip to the office and my conversation with my Mentor.

"I would love to go back, but I don't feel comfortable. I need a little more time. It was just fun seeing the place." I don't know why I lied. I was itching to get back to work.

"I've never known you to run from a challenge."

"I'm not running, but in my condition, do you think it's appropriate for me to just jump in without reviewing cases, or at least knowing peoples' names and faces? I'll look like an idiot!"

"This is a first."

"What?"

"Your being concerned about what people think of you."

"There's a first time for everything."

"Yeah, but this isn't the Kelsey I knew."

"I'm beginning to think that she is about as dead as the dog in my dreams."

Chapter Fourteen

Isabel and Moriah

T he next couple of days I kept to myself. Gregory was nice enough to take the boys down to his parent's house, giving me time to relax and unwind. The dream of my grandfather really sent me for a loop. I felt bad because I didn't have a chance to spend more time with him or further discuss what he had said. *It's time to grow up.* What did he mean by that? From what I can tell, before my episode, I was probably the most grown-up person I knew. It was weird that he referenced my age as being two. Had he been watching me from another dimension? Had he been the saving grace that helped protect me from my horrible car accident? And what the heck was his crazy obsession with *Stick Ups?*

With no real obligation to anyone, I found myself lying around the house trying to coerce myself to go to sleep hoping that my grandfather would come back and explain himself. However, nothing ever happened. As a matter of fact, it was the first time in weeks that I could remember dozing off and not having a dream at all. I was actually able to get some rest for a change!

As the day dragged on, I was able to catch up on some reading, work out, and cook myself a steak dinner with all the fixings. This was a treat for me since Gregory doesn't eat red meat, and it is rarely served to the children. It was a chance to do and be anything I wanted, but it was driving me crazy that I had no one to do it with. I came to the conclusion that I'm not too comfortable being by myself and found myself calling, of all the people in the world, my mother.

"Hi, Mom. What are you doing?" I asked.

"A little gardening. What are you doing today, Kelsey?"

"Nothing at the moment. Do you want to do something?"

"Oh, baby I would love to be with you, but I have plans to go to one of my club's charitable events this afternoon, and it will last until late this evening. Why don't you call Jamie and see if you two can do something together?" she suggested. Great. I'm pathetic; even my mom has more of a life than I do.

"Dr. Jamie? No thanks. I don't need her over analyzing me."

"You do realize that Jamie is not just your doctor, she's been your best friend for over twenty years."

"That's what I keep being told, but I don't feel like it. She's the one I go to unload, not hang out with."

"Kelsey, that's ridiculous."

"No, Mom, that's my truth. She's my doctor. Besides, I don't want to bother her."

"Why do you think you're bothersome?"

I only felt that way with Dr. Jamie. Gregory had no choice, and I wouldn't be able to shake Mom loose if I tried. However, with Dr. Jamie, from what she told me, she didn't have much of a life, and it seemed lately that my sessions with her were too taxing on the both of us.

"Mom, I'll let you go."

"Are you gonna be alright?"

"Sure, I will. I'll see what's playing at the movies," I told her as cheerfully as I could. I had just realized that if Mom thought I was lonely, she'd camp out on my doorstep. Sometimes she's more protective than Gregory; you'd think *they* were blood related. I'm convinced they're in cahoots.

"Have fun tonight."

"You do the same, dear."

I hung up the phone and stared at the front of the fridge for a good five minutes before I officially stated, "I am truly alone."

I have been so preoccupied with my condition that I forgot to make or keep friends? I had met, or rather, was *reintroduced* to a couple of women who I was told were my good friends I had known for years. However, like Gregory, when we all got together, I didn't feel like we had anything in common.

A few months after my accident, Jamie coordinated a brunch with all of my old friends. It was a very awkward gathering. One of my old friends was named Tonya, a tall, black woman with long legs, and long hair like me. Had I not known it, I would have assumed she was related to me. She was a stay-at-home mom of three and was married to a successful podiatrist. You would have thought this man was the second coming the way she went on and on about him. As she ran her mouth and pulled out a purse size picture book of her family, I could not pay attention to the photos or anything she said. Though she was pretty, Tonya spoke too loudly, had lipstick smeared across her big white-capped teeth, and she monopolized the conversation the entire time talking with her chewed food exposed. To think that Gregory tried to hit on her first the night we met. What did he see in this loud-talking, food smacking wildebeest?

Another friend of mine named Jennifer was a waif-like, platinum blonde haired, blue-eyed woman whose youthful looks would make you think she was about eighteen instead of thirty-two. She seemed really down to earth, but I think she consumed more alcohol than she did food. She kept shooting back shots of Tequila trying to get all of us to partake with her at 1pm. When we chose not to participate, she shrugged her shoulders and downed our shots as well as hers. Thank God she wasn't driving.

Then there was Zafirah. She was Middle Eastern, and I'm told we called her Zee because half of us couldn't remember how to properly pronounce her name. Though she was very attractive, she spent the entire time talking negatively about herself, her job, and she went on and on about how she would probably never get married like the rest of us. Dr. Jamie was kind enough to remind her that she wasn't married, but Zee just threw salt on an old wound, acknowledging that at least she was divorced. Dr. Jamie looked as if she could slap her. Zee rambled on about how she wasn't as successful or pretty as the rest of us; she was a complete downer. I, for one, couldn't even imagine hanging out with anyone that was there at brunch.

Everyone, except for Zee, wanted to extend our brunch into a long-winded chat session at Tonya's house. Jennifer offered to whip up a batch of her famous Margaritas while we rehashed the good ole days and recant how many hearts we collectively have broken over the years. I passed; I was too preoccupied with getting home. You see, I left my book of 20,000 names in another purse, and I couldn't wait to look up Zee's name. So much so, that I almost knocked Tommy down over rushing to get the book and would not answer his repeated calls. Zafirah meant "She who wins" in Arabic. *How ironic.* To hear Zee tell it, she was the biggest loser ever born.

Well, it's official…I have nobody that I call a friend. That thought drove me to the freezer to get a pint of Haagen-Dazs rum raisin ice cream. I turned on the television, put on an old black and white movie, and fiercely shoved the spoon into my mouth. I inhaled half a pint before bursting into tears. There's nothing like having a pity party over ice cream. I must have been a sight. Since I was still too mad to call my Mentor, I cried myself to sleep instead.

When I realized that I was back in the woods, I somehow felt relieved. At least it was something to do. I actually hugged one of the trees and stood there drinking in the warm sunshine that was peeking through the trees. I breathed in deeply the fragrant scent of the fresh morning rain; it was spring. I could see the leaves on the tree limbs were budding, and it made me excited. It felt as if change or hope was in the air.

As I walked around the forest, I soaked up the melodic sound of birds chirping. What was usually a hellishly dark and gloomy terrain seemed more like a pleasant day for a hike or a picnic today. I started to weave in and out of the trees dancing and twirling around, bumping dizzily into their brownish bark. They seemed to welcome my giggles as I swirled faster and faster until I was laughing out of control. When I could no longer stand, I laid on the ground staring up into the cloudless blue sky. It was a beautiful day.

I closed my eyes and felt totally at peace; one with nature, and one with God. I was in my own little world for so long that I didn't hear that someone was standing directly over me. If it weren't for the edge of the hemline on their clothing grazing my hairline, I might not have known they were there at all. When I felt the faint brush of material across my nose, I almost freaked out, but instead, I froze. I was too scared to open my eyes to see what was hovering over me. Whatever it was, I knew it wasn't an animal.

"Is she dead?"

"I don't think so."

"Why is she lying down?"

"Why does anyone do anything?"

"I think she's weird."

"You think everyone is weird. I think she's just resting."

I got up enough courage to peek through my long lashes to see what was above me. Their voices were that of children, but I could tell they were women. I could not see much with my left eye as the glare of the sunlight pierced my pupil. With one quick motion, I decided to open both eyes, and when I did, I saw two angelic faces gazing directly at mine. I quickly sat up, trying to gain focus, but I was temporarily blinded by the beam of sunshine that was illuminating from over their heads. I must have had my eyes closed longer than it seemed.

"What do you want?" I asked swinging my arms wildly and waiting for my eyes to gain focus to see who was standing in front of me.

"Nothing you have," one of them replied.

"Isabel, that was rude!" the other scolded.

"What'd I say?"

"Are you alright? You were laying there…we couldn't tell if you were hurt or not. We just saw a dead dog a while back and wanted to make sure you were okay." My eyes finally adjusted, and I was able to see a round-faced woman with piercing blue eyes staring at me. Her face was warm, and she looked as if she was truly concerned.

"I was just taking in some rays," I answered her.

"Rays of what?" the other one questioned. She was standing behind her friend and was looking inquisitively at me. Her face was exquisite. Not as round as her friend, she had sharp features, big, expressive, pale-blue eyes, and freckles.

"The sun was hitting my face and it felt good." They didn't answer so I continued. "I'm Kelsey, what's your name?"

"I'm Moriah and she is Isabel."

"Are you stuck in the woods, too?" They looked at each other as if I were speaking an alien dialect.

"Let me help you up," Moriah said as she extended me a hand.

"Thank you."

That was the way I met what would later become my closest confidants. After that weekend, Isabel and Moriah would visit me in my dreams often. It was great to be able to discuss my wildest thoughts and darkest fears without having someone trying to over analyze them the way Dr. Jamie did. I could unload my fears and discuss my utmost desires with them, and they never seemed to judge me. They would listen intently and then tell me of their experiences without judging me. They also kept me company as I wandered in the wilderness. If they did offer their advice, it was sound and soothing. Both were personable, but Isabel had a matter-of-fact, no-nonsense attitude towards life and men. She saw things as either black or white; gray did not exist. I could identify with her the most because sometimes I feel as if I spend more time thinking about what I really want to say but am constantly biting my tongue. Alright, so maybe I don't bite my tongue as much as I would like to, but I'm a work in progress. Like her sharp features, Isabel was tall and lanky, and her long brown hair fell softly off of her shoulders.

Moriah, on the other hand, was the one who was the sensitive one in our little group. She had curly locks that made her look like a little cherub, and her rosy wide cheeks were radiant and always glowing. She was the one who peppered her speech with compliments, always made me look at the bright side on any given topic, and her smile was enormously comforting. They made my tireless nights in the woods a delight.

When I told Gregory about my two new friends, he looked as if he wanted to have me committed right then and there. I just laughed and giggled. So, what if he thought I was crazy. They validated the fact that I wasn't, especially when it came to discussing things regarding him.

"Gregory thinks I'm crazy because you are my friends," I confessed one day.

"Do you think you're crazy, Kelsey?" Moriah asked.

"Not at all."

"I'll never understand men," Isabel interjected. "They don't appreciate anything, want to take credit for everything, but don't want to take the blame when it is called for."

"What do you mean?" I asked.

"The problems of the world today are because men won't stand up and acknowledge their mistakes, atone, and try to do it better. They rely mostly on their own strength, and to just be frank…"

"Please, Isabel, be frank," Moriah teased.

"They just don't get it."

"There has to be men out there that are capable of doing what you just described," I suggested.

"Not without being taught. Everybody is too smart nowadays. Gone are the days of people wanting to be taught or are teachable. Plus, like I mentioned, no one is grateful for anything," she replied. I have to admit I didn't understand half of what she was saying.

Isabel had a habit of going off on little rants, so I changed the subject. "Well, Gregory can be extremely smothering at times. I know that he's trying to be nice, but I'm not able to respond to him the way that he would like me to. Even when I try, he always does something to mess up the moment," I complained and briefly told them about the birthday flower fiasco.

"Could you not appreciate the sentiment of the gift?" Moriah asked.

"Oh no, these flowers were too ugly to be appreciated. Besides, I don't want that type of insincere gesture to be embedded into my sons' psyche. Better for them to learn now what we women really want. Right?" I replied.

"See! That's exactly what I've been talking about!" Isabel exclaimed.

Chapter Fifteen

Where's My Father?

As much as I liked Isabel, sometimes I felt as if her comments were directed towards me. Even though she never said so and wasn't unkind, statements like that one made me feel uneasy.

"Are you saying that I was ungrateful?" I questioned Dr. Jamie at our next session when she told me her opinion on the matter of Gregory's flowers.

"Yes. You weren't thankful that your husband took the time to buy you flowers. That's more that some women get," she commented.

Since she answered the way that she did, I decided not to tell her about my two new friends.

"Sometimes, I swear you, and Gregory are in cahoots," I proclaimed.

"Do you say that because you think I'm on Gregory's side, or because you think I should always agree with your behavior?"

"It's just hard for me to believe that we were ever close friends."

"Being your close friend has nothing to do with my having sound thinking," she answered with an attitude. So, I got snippy.

"Dr. Jamie, are you saying my thinking is not sound just because it is different from yours?"

"No, I'm saying that just because I don't think the way you do on many occasions doesn't mean that I am incapable of being your best friend. Actually, it might be the reason that we were such good friends. Kelsey, you have always been strong-willed and strong-minded. However, you were never interested in anyone or anything that couldn't mentally challenge you. Keep that in mind when we talk because I am simply being who I have always been to you—a truthful friend. Most people were cowardice in your presence."

"Is that true with Gregory?"

"It's not like he was henpecked or anything, but you do have a strong personality and have a way of getting what you wanted. He liked letting you have your way, but you also knew when not to cross the line."

"Have I changed so much that I can't see that line anymore?"

"Yes."

"How do I go back so that I'm not like who I am now?" "I don't believe you should."

"Meaning?" I asked truly wanting to know her opinion on this subject.

"I believe you are at a point in your life where you can become better than what you used to be. That's why I have been encouraging you to move forward with your life, instead of always looking back," she responded.

"I know that I am rough around the edges, but part of me doesn't think or feel as if I need to change. Is it possible that this is who I was always meant to be?"

"Finding out what is truth and what is not will be the most challenging part of your ordeal."

"So, tell me, how do you change something you don't believe is broken?"

"The answer to that question will come when you can decipher what will make you a better person once you find out the characteristics that hinder you from living a full and complete life," she added.

"As I have been saying all along until I know, or can remember who I was, I won't be able to find the answers. Though you all are helpful, Dr. Jamie, I can no longer rely on what you and others tell me. That's why I want to remember things for myself so I can decide what needs to be changed," I concluded.

Dr. Jamie stared at me for a while before she flatly announced, "Times up. I'll see you next week."

After my appointment with Dr. Jamie, I had a chance to grab lunch at a little café down the street. It was a beautiful warm summer afternoon with a slight breeze. A perfect day to sit outside and people watch. As I sat nursing a Mimosa, I watched a thirty-something-year-old man playing with his preschool-aged daughter. Her little hand was tucked safely in his as they skipped down the street. She was darling with reddish-brown ringlets and she wore a pale yellow and purple gingham dress which brought to mind a few baby pictures in which Ms. Kerri-Claire used to dress me in similar types of outfits. Unlike me, she looked lovely in hers. I saw how attentive this preppy-dressed man was with his little princess, and tears welled up in my eyes. I wanted to remember that if it ever existed.

I hadn't forgotten that Mom still had not produced the evidence that she even knew my father. It was always in the back of my mind and I was silently counting down the days, waiting to see if she would honor her word and produce the evidence. Personally, I never believed that she had any photos, but I would like to believe that my own mother hadn't lied to me. Some would say that it shouldn't matter if my father was around or whether his relationship lasted with my mother. I believe that might be true. However, it's the lie and the false hope my mother continues foster in me that makes me not let the subject go. Understanding the birds and bees, I don't need to be convinced that he was real; I just would like to see what he looked like, connect with him the same way I did with my grandfather.

If nothing else, this nightmare has taught me to appreciate my history. It's like putting all of a puzzle's edges together before working on the middle. As I look at the puzzle of my life, there are so many edges missing that I don't know where to start in order to finish it.

My session today with Dr. Jamie confirmed that point. I have grown so comfortable in this skin that if I had to live in it for the rest of my life that it would probably be fine. However, I don't want to. *What is it that you want, Kelsey?* I want it all: the whole kit and caboodle. I want to have my memory back. I want a strong marriage, if not with Gregory, then with the man I'm supposed to be with. Blessed kids, a healthy and truthful relationship with my mother, and I want to be a good friend. That's not asking too much, is it? As I sat there soaking up the sunshine, I hit one of the speed dial numbers that was programmed into my phone.

"Sorry we haven't spoken in a while," I said to my Mentor. It was the only way I could think of how to apologize for our last conversation when I got angry and rushed him off the phone.

"I missed talking to you. How has everything been?"

I quickly brought him up to speed and told him about my new friends, the man, and his daughter, and wanting to be whole again.

"Do you think you were ever whole?" he inquired. That was a good question. I had never thought about it that way.

"Do you mean, I think my life was perfect before?" I asked stalling for time so I could figure out how to answer his question.

"You know what I mean. You just gave me a laundry list of things you ultimately wanted to obtain. That would leave me to believe that they didn't exist before."

"I guess so."

"What has everybody been constantly telling you about your past?"

"That I was successful, a good mother, and a loving wife. A good friend to Dr. Jamie and close with my mom. Why?"

"Well, if you used to be all of those things, then wouldn't that mean you still are?" I knew he was setting me up for some Jedi mind trick; I just couldn't see which way it was coming from.

"I suppose," I offered meekly.

"Well, if that is so, why is your best friend constantly trying to get you to change?"

"Is she asking me to change or trying to get me out of my current rut?"

"You just said she wanted you to be happy and healthy right?"

"Uh-huh."

"Why would she want you to be those things if you already were?

Wouldn't she want you to be happy and healthy the way you used to be?" It was a good question, and I had no answer.

"Maybe it's because I'm the one that's on a soul-searching pilgrimage and since my accident, I have not been my normal self," I stated still not fully knowing where he was going.

"Something's out of joint, Kelsey. Your mom insists that you were very tight-knit, but you can sense she is lying. You told me before that you don't seem remotely connected with your old girlfriends in any shape or fashion. Your husband pretty much repulses you, and you believe you have to change? Sounds like you have to get to the bottom of some serious matters to see if it is time to either confront some old issues or release them. Sweeping things under the rug to move forward so that it is convenient for others is not the way to go."

He was right. Why was I wasting my time defending everyone in my life? His whole conversation sounded as if he knew something about everyone that I didn't. Something isn't right. I made up my mind to do the most sensible thing by delving into the recesses of myself so I could move onward, but he made me feel as if I were right where I needed to be.

"Before you start changing yourself, try analyzing those in your life. It will help you to gain a greater perspective of your loved ones. In any relationship there has to be compromise, something you need to learn, missy. Understand that two people can't coexist, be it a business partnership or a healthy relationship, unless they can agree on one common ground. You agreeing to become something that your soul is telling you doesn't seem right would be a big mistake, you understand?" I nodded and I think he could sense that I was dizzy from all of his advice.

"What I'm saying is take your time. Instead of rushing forward too quickly, Kelsey, you need to identify what you know and assess if you believe it is the truth."

"So, do you think everyone's being deceitful?"

"What I'm saying is that everybody has a motive for everything. Especially those who love us the most, and their view may be slanted. However, sometimes there needs to be a little chaos in life in order to desire to restore it with peace. I think that was the significance of your accident; getting others no to rely on you so much."

Wow. My head was spinning from all of the words of wisdom. I swear I could use a nap.

"Give it some thought, Kelsey. I'll talk to you in a couple of days."

"Before you go, let me ask you a question. Since you knew my grandfather so well, did he ever say anything to you about my father, or did you ever meet him?" I don't know why I never thought to ask him before.

"Kelsey, I had seen your father around from time to time, but I did not know him, and if he saw me today, I don't think he would know me either."

Just like I thought, my phone call to my mom a couple of weeks ago prompted Ms. Kerri-Claire to spring into smother mode. She went out of her way to plan several mother-daughter weekends and outings. The first one she planned for us was at an all-day spa, which I did appreciate.

"Baby, do you remember Ethereal? This used to be your favorite place to unwind," my mother said.

When I walked into the beautiful and serene establishment, I could feel its refreshing and soothing atmosphere wrap itself around me. Though I didn't remember how the place looked, I did feel as if I had been here before. My mother treated me to a full day of beauty treatments. It was wonderful to sit and let people rejuvenate you over with backrubs, relaxing soaks, scrubs, and hair treatments. I was in heaven.

As the masseur worked on my knotted back and body muscles, I could faintly sense the life flowing back into my unresponsive body. For over two years, this corpse of mine has walked around void of feelings. Hector kneaded away my worries; I am embarrassed to say that I actually longed for my husband's touch.

I left Ethereal feeling refreshed and stress-free, but after my conversation with my Mentor, there was no way I was gonna let Mom off the hook; I had some questions to ask her regarding my father. I almost didn't want to ruin the lovely day we had together, but I couldn't wait until we got into the car.

"Mom, will you ever tell me the truth about my father?" I asked as sweet as I could. She didn't say much for a long time. Then she began with a whole new lie.

"Kelsey, your father didn't die, we got divorced when you were young, and I haven't seen him since."

"Mom, cut the crap! Do you think I'm that dumb? I had already hired someone to check out the info you gave me!" It was true; the weekend that I was alone in the house, I went through everything in my home office and found a file folder tucked in back of one of the file cabinets. Apparently, months before my accident I had hired a company to search for my dad. The name, birth date, and city of origin had all come back inconclusive. She sat in the passenger seat with her mouth hanging open; we obviously shared that same trait.

"You hired a private detective to search for your father?"

"Apparently. So, you have a couple of choices to make. Either tell me the truth, give me the right name, or else," I demanded. She just sat there for a long time without saying anything.

"How about it, Mom?" I gave her one last chance to tell me the truth as we pulled up in front of her house.

"Kelsey, I just don't want to talk about it. I know you have the right to know what happened regarding your father, but he is just as much my memory as he is yours, and I am in no mood to deal with this right now."

Chapter Sixteen

The More I Look at Gregory

By the time I came home from dropping my mother off, all newfound feelings towards Gregory had vanished. I knew that as soon as my mother got in the door, the first call she would make would be to her precious son-in-law. Sure enough, there he was lounging on the couch with his leg up on the back of the sofa consoling her. What a momma's boy!

By the time I put down my stuff and walked into the kitchen for a cool drink, he was there ready to defend her. I swear you'd think *they* were married the way they always tag-teamed me.

"What?" I asked before he started up.

"I was just gonna ask if you were okay."

"Ah-hah."

"Mom sounded really upset, so I figured you would be, too."

"Ah-hah," I replied again as I moved around our large gourmet kitchen.

"Kelsey, why didn't you tell me that you hired a private investigator?"

"I didn't know that I did until I found a file in my office," I replied frankly.

"What file?" he asked nervously with his eyes wide. I walked casually into my office, grabbed the file off the desk, and placed it on the counter for him to thumb through. After reviewing its contents, he responded.

"I'm sorry this led to a dead end. I know how important finding information regarding your father has always meant to you." Why was he being so nice?

"Thanks. It doesn't look like I'm gonna find out much from her now. That's too bad because I thought we were finally becoming closer." I baited him with a little white lie. That's the third time I had openly fibbed about something in the past two months. That's normally not like me, and I better make a mental note to cut it out.

"Let me talk to her. She's pretty upset right now. She mentioned you had a wonderful day together, so your questioning her threw her off guard."

The next day when I had a session with Dr. Jamie, I asked her, "Did I ever tell you that I hired an investigator to look for my father?"

"What?" I guess not the way she responded, she was truly surprised. She continued, "Really? When?"

"Yep, a few months before my accident. I found a file in my home office desk drawer."

"What did they find out? Is he still alive—do tell?" She was more excited than I had anticipated.

"Zero. We don't believe she gave us the right information about him. So basically, everything I had been told about my father was not true. Why should I believe that my mother is telling me the truth about my dad now? I thought my dad's name was Jay Smith and it isn't."

"That's deep."

"When I confronted Ms. Kerri-Claire about the situation, she made up another lie."

"You told her! No wonder I got six messages from her last night. It's a good thing I wasn't home," she sounded relieved.

"She's probably called everyone in the family to discuss our conversation, and Debbie Martin, too. I could barely get the key in the door, and she was already on the phone with Gregory pleading her case."

"What did Gregory say?"

"He was actually very supportive of me. I told him I was very upset about the whole situation seeing that how we were getting along so well lately. He said he would talk to her to see if she would finally tell the truth." That was a strategic seed planted for Jamie in case she spoke with my mother. "You know, it was weird, but I could have sworn that Gregory was acting a little nervous when he found out that I had hired an investigator."

"Did he really?" she asked coolly. Actually, too coolly. "Yep."

"Why do you think he would be nervous about that?" Dr. Jamie inquired.

"I don't know. Maybe he has something to hide," I answered, never thinking about it before. Did Gregory have something to hide?

Later that evening the family spent a nice quiet evening at home. I made my famous chicken Paella, mango salad with freshly baked bread, and my boys gobbled it up for once without a fight.

"Mommy, look, I ate all of my salad," Tommy proudly proclaimed.

"That's a good little dinosaur," I praised him.

Normally, I have to go WWF on him to get him to eat any kind of vegetables. The two of us would go nine rounds, and it would take him over an hour to finish a side helping of corn. One day, I had to put my foot down and boldly announce, "Look child, I do not negotiate with terrorists! Sit and eat your vegetables. NOW!" It took two years to get it to sink in, but he's doing much better now. I even taught the boys our new household mantra, "A Happy Mommy Is a Happy Family!" Words to live by or die. While the kids were upstairs playing with Joanna, I asked Gregory if he had a chance to speak with my mom.

"Not yet. I'm waiting for the right moment," he light-heartedly responded. Was he serious?

"Well, when do you plan to ask her? After she makes up another cockamamie story or after she's dead?" Why, is it that no one shares my sense of urgency?

"Kels, I didn't think it was that big of a deal," he said looking at me like a stupid puppy dog.

"You said it yourself that after she called, you knew how important finding out anything regarding my father was to me! Why all of a sudden it is no big deal?" I asked raising my voice. One of the kids must have thought that I was calling them because Jesse came running into the family room.

"Yes, Mommy?" he said politely.

"Sorry, baby, Mommy didn't call you. I was talking to Daddy."

"I heard you all the way upstairs. Were you yelling at daddy? Are you guys gonna get a divorce?"

"Who taught you a big word like that?" Gregory asked. "I'm not a little boy you know," Jesse responded.

"Yes, you are, buddy!" Gregory stated as he scooped the tyke up in his arms to reassure him and whisked him off upstairs.

It's moments like this that Gregory can be so endearing. Yet, on other occasions, the more I look at Gregory, the more I have to question, *what I was thinking marrying this man? Did I pregnant and forced him into a shotgun wedding? How drunk was I to lay down with this man in the first place?* It seems as if we have nothing in common. He's a sports fanatic; I could care less about any sport. He has a lot of close friends, but from what I can tell, I only had one, and I'm not that close with her anymore. He likes to move around; I love to relax and chill. I love to read books; he can't sit still long enough to finish a magazine. They say opposites attract, but I don't get it. Whatever Vulcan's mind trick he played on me must have worked because there is no way in a million years that would I have chosen this man to live with for the rest of my life.

"I'm sorry, Kels, I wanted to give her a day to calm down, and I forgot to follow up. Forgive me?" he pleaded as he strolled back into the family room.

"Thirty lashings for you, sailor," I flirted. There's nothing sexier than a confession.

Chapter Seventeen

Mi Bambinos

When I told my Mentor about my little tiff with Gregory, he asked a question I never considered.

"Kelsey, do you want more children?"

"Where did that come from? I hadn't thought about it."

"The thought of having a daughter never crossed your mind?" Why was he snooping?

"I guess I've been spending so much time trying to get a handle on the two it never did cross my mind."

"You would be great with a little girl."

"You think? I have to admit the boys have really grown on me. They are too adorable. Tommy, the youngest one, is a complete mess. The things that come out of his little inquisitive mouth are too precious."

"I think you should try for another," he boldly pronounced.

"I think it would be best if I get to know their father a little bit more, don't you?"

"What's to know?"

"Something's just not clicking. My body doesn't respond to him at all."

"He's your husband, Kelsey; just let it be."

"I have the strangest feeling that he's either up to something, or he's hiding something."

"Could it be that he's just nice?"

"No one's that nice," I stated suspiciously.

"That's the problem with you young women today. You always need an explanation for something. You married him, he's there trying his hardest to please you, be a wife to him. That's your responsibility."

I can't begin to tell you how awkward it was to receive marital instructions from an older man. It was downright disturbing. If I could be assured that I would have replicas of Jesse and Tommy, I'd have forty children. They have become my saving grace over the years; they have matured a little and are actually so much fun to have around. I love throwing them in the car and taking off on adventures in the middle of the day.

Sometimes, I offer to pick them up from school and we race off to get ice cream or baseball cards, and when we return, we are full of sniggles. Joanna must think we are crazy, but we sit around the kitchen table making weird noises trying to see who can be the weirdest. They have quickly become the reason I get up in the morning, and I'm their biggest, best mommy. They give me peace of mind in a time of uncertainty, and I find myself being more relaxed around them.

Jesse said that he had forgiven me for not remembering that he didn't like jelly, and I forgave him for being disrespectful. They were constantly making me gifts at school and rushing them home trying to outdo each other.

"Mommy, look what I made you!" Jesse exclaimed proudly, showing off a handmade picture frame that was decorated with beads and dried noodles.

"That is lovely. Good job, honey."

"I made you something, too, Mommy." Tommy started to fake cry in order to get my attention.

"Mommy, he's faking!"

"No, I'm not," Tommy replied straight-faced.

"What did you make me Tommy?"

"He didn't make anything. I told you he's faking," Jesse busted him.

"Yes, I did. It's a make-believe gift. See, Mommy?" Tommy stuck out his tongue at his big brother.

"Wow, that's amazing. You mean I got two gifts today and I didn't have to do anything for them. Is it my birthday?" I asked wide- eyed and making a funny face.

"No!" they squealed unison.

"Are you sure?"

"Yep guys …we just love you," Tommy admitted.

"Well, I love you, too. Thank you for making them, and thanks for making me a mommy."

"You're welcome, Mom," Jesse told me.

"I don't think I can adequately describe how my kids have given meaning to my life. I want to be the best I can be for them," I confessed.

"Kelsey, I do understand. They are my godchildren, and they should be cherished," Dr. Jamie said.

"Did I ever want a girl?"

"You never mentioned it to me. Thinking of having more?"

"No, I was just curious. Hanging out with the two of them, it's hard not to consider having more. Joanna has done a great job with them."

"Don't sell yourself short; you raised those boys. Joanna was your backup if you needed them picked up or looked after if you had a meeting."

"You're kidding?"

"No, I'm not. What you are feeling is a result of what you cultivated in them? It only feels new to you because you don't remember the work, patience, and love you have extended into them."

"You mean I had a hand in that? A hand in them turning out to be so amazing?" I asked in disbelief.

"Actually, it was all you! Gregory spent most of his time out with the boys or trying to generate sales at work. You are the wind beneath your boys' wings, and that's why they are responding to you the way they have."

All I could do was weep. I had finally done something right.

Chapter Eighteen

Three Years Old

"This year I want to be completely healed!" I proclaimed as I blew out the three candles on an oversized piece of key lime cheesecake.

I continued, "I'm tired of spending every night in the forest; tired of not getting answers, and tired of feeling incomplete as a person." I was conversing as if I had a roomful of witnesses, but the truth is, it was just me in the massive penthouse suite in the Eden Roc Resort & Spa in Miami.

Things had been so tense in all of my relationships that for my 3rd birthday, I wanted to take a relaxing getaway by myself. Not working every day for the past three years should have been relaxing in itself but, to tell you the truth, it wasn't. I was barely able to survive last year. My relationship with my mother is almost nonexistent, and she refuses to give me any information about my father. It's been a few months since we have spoken. The thought of growing closer to Gregory has become a pipedream; he is constantly irritating me by smothering me. Not to mention, he has proven to be no help with my mother. Lastly, Dr. Jamie has mentioned on several occasions that I looked exhausted and if I have lost too much weight.

My only saving grace is my babies. Still, they cannot fill the void in my life. Even my relationship with my Mentor has taken a turn for the worst. Chugging down a glass of cold water, I began to reflect over the past two months.

⎯⊷⊶⎯

It all started a few months ago when I resumed my position in the woods and started to think of the dead dog again. probably because I was standing in the spot where I thought I had found it, but it was no longer there. In the distance, I could hear a dog barking, and as it caught my attention, I began to walk in the direction of its echo. I spotted the pooch up ahead, and as I approached it, it never occurred to me that the canine might be dangerous. So, when it attacked my arm, I was completely caught off guard. The voracious mutt clung onto my arm, and all I could do was swing my arm wildly hoping that it would get dizzy and let go. Not a chance. The more I swung, the tighter its grip became around my arm, causing my sleeve to stain with blood. The only way that I was able to get loose from its clutches was to smack it against hard a tree trunk; had I not, it would have chewed through my entire limb.

It yelped as it fell and ran off in the opposite direction to avoid getting struck again. Feeling no pain whatsoever, I was so mad that I gave chase. Yelling after it, I ran at top speed, and at one point, I even ran past the four-legged creature. When I turned to catch it, it stopped in its tracks and "poof" turned into burning flames. I stood there watching as it burned to a crisp. I ran my fingers over my ravaged forearm, but when I looked down, my arm was completely healed. All I could do was stand frozen in my tracks staring in awe at the locale of charred ashes.

"What do you think the dream meant?" I asked Isabel who was staring at me as if she had a big secret. "It was your dream. That is for you to find out," she coldly replied.

"Kelsey, you're smart. What do you think it meant?" Moriah asked.

"Sometimes I think the dog is either my mom or Gregory and that they are out to get me. Then other times, I just don't know."

"What do you think is out to get you?" Isabel's eyes turned dull and sinister as she asked the question.

"Don't you mean *who?*"

"No, I asked the question, right? *What* do you think is out to get you?"

"Maybe they are memories that are trying to come back, but I cannot let them?"

Dr. Jamie looked at me as if she were going to commit me right there on the spot when I finally told her about Isabel and Moriah visiting me in my dreams. Though her expression was blank, color rushed through her cheeks as if she were about to explode. She let out a deep sigh before she spoke.

"Kelsey, what do you think your two friends represent in your dreams?"

"I think they represent themselves."

"So, you think these women actually exist?"

"They don't just exist, they are my friends," I answered, surprised at her tone.

"Kelsey, have you considered that they aren't real people? I mean, where did they come from? How did they get in your dreams?"

"I don't know, but it would be no different than if you or Gregory were in my dreams!" I defended.

"I think it's very different. You know Gregory and me!" she shouted back.

"So, what if I don't know them personally. I believe they are out there somewhere. How do you know that I didn't know them before my accident?"

"I would have known if you did."

"Are you saying I didn't do anything without you?" "That's right!"

"So, we were sown at the hip? There is no chance that, with all the people I knew—my clients, other lawyers—that Isabel or Moriah isn't someone that you DIDN'T know?" I yelled back at her.

"Anything is possible, Kelsey," she answered defeated.

"What difference does it make? I finally have someone that I can talk to. Should I feel guilty for that?"

"No, Kelsey, it's your world, I guess."

"What does that mean?"

"It means that as long as you make up the rules, nothing else matters."

What was the big deal? Why was she so mad at me? Had I done something wrong? I mulled it over in my head all the way home. I need to talk to somebody. Gregory was at work and wouldn't be interested. No use in calling my mom. My Mentor. I picked up the phone as it was ringing.

"Hello."

"Hey, stranger."

"I was about to call you—I miss you. Where has my favorite superhero been?"

"Out saving the world, baby girl, out saving the world. What's up?"

"It seems like every time I call you I've got a problem." "I don't mind."

I rehashed my dream and conversation with Dr. Jamie, and he listened quietly.

"I tell you; I don't know what she wants from me." "What does anyone want?"

"I'm learning to stop guessing. You'll have to tell me." "Love. Jamie is very lonely. You should be nicer to her."

"I am nice to her, but I feel as if she wants something from me that I can't give. Besides, she's my oldest friend; she knows the truth about several areas in my life and she won't even tell me what she knows."

"So, are you holding your friendship hostage?"

"Not at all! Can't she see I'm hurting? She is holding so many keys, and she won't share." I sounded like a three-year-old for sure with that last statement.

"Kelsey, did it ever occur to you that maybe you are the only one who can walk out this journey?"

"It's too much to bear sometimes. Too many things to juggle. Sometimes I just want to kill myself because I can't take all the constant pressure."

"Don't talk like that. You have too much to live for; more than most people."

"I know, but what good is it to be in a great big house and never feel loved."

"Are you serious? You have love oozing out of your ears. What else do you need?"

"The truth."

"What *is* truth? What you perceive to be real, or what you want to be real?"

"I just want what *is true*. That's not too much to ask for. If I can get what *is real*, I can begin dealing with what to or not to change. How to live and how to love those in my life. Without truth, I'm left in the dark."

"What if what "is" is what you are in right now?"

"That's like telling me to release everything that I want to know and move forward."

"Exactly!"

"Why? Do you think I can't handle the past?"

"About as much as you could keep that dog off of you.

"Ha! But I got it off of me, and then ran it down," I boasted.

"Good. Now chase down your future," he concluded.

Every time I had a conversation with someone, it ended up just like that, a round of tit-for-tat. It has become extremely draining. My sessions with Dr. Jamie have resulted in me telling her what I think she wants me to say just so I don't have to hear her mouth. When I try to contact my Mentor, he's never available. I haven't had much of an appetite lately, and Gregory has been forcing me to eat, which usually ends up with us getting into a fight.

"Kels, you are looking too thin. You have to eat."

"I'm not very hungry; I'll eat something later."

"Kelsey, is something wrong? All you have been doing lately is sleeping and moping around the house. Baby, talk to me," he pleaded.

"Gregory, it's nothing, I just have a lot on my mind. I'll be okay."

"Know that I'm here for you if you need me to be. Any time of day or night, just come to me, I want to be your best friend. You don't have to keep things from me, Kelsey. It's obvious that you're doing some heavy thinking. Let me in. Maybe we should take a vacation," he said as he put his arms around me.

I didn't need a hug, I wanted answers. Answers he was not able to get out of Ms. Kerri-Claire.

"Did Mom ever tell you anything about my father?" Fess up.

"She still won't talk about it."

I was too tired to make a big fuss, but he is incapable of doing anything I need him to do.

Chapter Nineteen

The Pity Party

Reflecting on a montage of disappointments during the last year, even for these brief moments, was really disheartening. How can a man constantly tell you he loves you but won't do what you need him to do to prove his love? I need less talk and more action. The more I think about it, the more the tears came streaming down my face. For months, Gregory had been avoiding speaking to my mother, and each day he didn't assist me with my quest, I began to despise him even more. Every time I looked at him with that goofy puppy dog face, it was as if he were stabbing the knife in my back deeper. Nobody cares. I have been here for over 40 hours, and my phone did not ring once.

I understand that it was my idea to get away alone, but I did think they would call to check up on me. I've been laying here thinking about the last three years, and to tell you the truth, my existence doesn't add up to much. I've accumulated a lot of stuff, but I have nothing that I can say would make me want to stay in this dimension. My kids would be better off with the memories they have of me instead of my continually falling deeper into this funk. I've been thinking a lot about suicide lately. I was close on several occasions when I was left home feeling despondent. However, I could never hurt myself in the house because I feared one of the kids would find me. The thought of the light in Tommy's eyes fading fast as he discovered his Mother T-Rex's bloated body submerged in a bloody bath makes me sick. I could never do that to them in a million years no matter how dejected I felt. If I were to take my own life, I would do it in a place like here at The Eden Roc. I wouldn't care if the maid found me. I would just leave her a $50 tip and my mind would be at rest because I wouldn't have to worry about my kids being afraid of living in their own house.

How would you do it, Kelsey? I would only do it on a day like today—the last day of my stay. I would get fully made up like I am right now—my make-up was flawless. I took my time and curled my long locks in big loopy ringlets, so that when they took pictures of my lifeless body, I would at least look good. I would slip into one of the most elegant gowns that I brought with me on this trip, complete with matching stockings and shoes so Gregory would know how I should look for my open-casket funeral. I brought my best jewelry with me so that I could add the appropriate accessories. I wouldn't want to leave that to chance or some tasteless mortician. I would strategically place a notecard from my personalized stationery with two uncomplicated words on it on the pillow next to my head. It would read in purple or maybe in green ink: *Simply Misunderstood.*

Lastly, I would pack all of my belongings in my leather overnight bag and place them near the front door of my penthouse suite. I wouldn't want my things scattered all over the place. They should be neat and in order, so time at the crime scene would be minimal. Open and shut. Once I was dressed to my liking, I would simply slip myself a cocktail of prescription pills and go to sleep. I would do something brave and classy like that. I'm tired of all the tears, the emptiness, brokenness, and not fully understanding the *why*. I just want to go far away from this existence. I pray that my kids remember how much they made me smile and the sound of my mommy dinosaur growl. I pray that my mom would finally tell someone the truth about my dad, or even better, I want my dad to come to my memorial service. I want him to hear how I searched for his identity for years, break down in tears at my funeral, distressed because he never took the time to get to know me.

"And I want to get out of the woods," I murmured as I put on the last layer of lipstick over my pencil-traced lips. I can't figure out if

I'm not right for Gregory or if he is not right for me. I wish he finds the person who can love him the way he desires to be loved. For Dr. Jamie, I pray that she gets a life, a man, and some friends she can analyze around the clock. I give up on that job. She hasn't helped me one bit. Either she's a horrible doctor or a horrible friend.

I gave myself the once over trying desperately to stop crying, but nothing seems to work. *This is it, kiddo.* With one strong sniff, I stood, dabbed my make-up one last time, walked to the desk in the room and prepared to write out my two little words.

"Okay, will it be the purple or the green pen?" my own voice startled me. I closed my eyes and picked up a pen. Purple it is. I scribbled my message in perfect penmanship and walked over to what would have been Gregory's side of the bed and placed it on the pillow. The tears were flowing freely again, but I was determined not to mess up my makeup. I rushed quickly to the dressing area, dabbed my eyes again, and fanned vigorously with my hands. Now is not the time to cry, Kelsey. You are almost home. Once I had gained control over my tear ducts I was ready, but I couldn't move. No matter how hard I tried, I could not make my long limbs budge. *If only someone would have called today.*

"It doesn't matter now; my mind is made up, and it's too late," I said with finality.

My stubborn legs began to move, and I found myself ready to slip on top of the perfectly made bed. My prescription drug cocktail had already been prepared, and a couple of gulps were all it would take, I thought. I picked up the glass, said my name for the last time, "Kelsey Smith-Pritchard," and put the glass to my lips, but as I slowly opened my mouth, a faint chirping sound came from across the room. I closed my eyes trying to ignore it because I was mentally ready to quickly down the witch's brew when I heard that chirping sound again. This time it was louder, causing me to pause. I immediately recognized the assigned ring tone. I slammed the glass down and jumped up to get my purse so that I wouldn't miss the call. As I fumbled through my clutch bag for my miniature cell phone, I quickly pressed the *Send* button. Before I could say "Hello," the caller began speaking.

"How's the birthday weekend going, Kelsey? Are you having fun relaxing?" my Mentor asked, as if he already knew the answer. I began to uncontrollably sob. He had done it again. He was truly my savior.

Chapter Twenty

Their Conversations

It had been over three years since Kelsey began seeing Jamie after her car accident. Though there had been minimal growth, Jamie had concerns that Kelsey's personality had become grossly dark. She could sense that her friend's tepid demeanor was masking a murky side of insecurities. Jamie had observed her carefully in their sessions and knew that Kelsey wasn't being completely honest with her. The tension in the air could be cut with a knife. As a therapist, Jamie had been trained to recognize when a patient was going through the motions during a session, and when they were truly trying to uncover new areas in their lives. Kelsey's session had become a rest stop for her.

In their previous sessions, Kelsey's starry-eyed enthusiasm for her newfound friends had deeply concerned Jamie. However, now Kelsey's enthusiasm had been replaced with short answers if any were given at all. With every question Jamie posed, Kelsey seemed to be searching or concocting the perfect response. Her smile was forced, and her body language standoffish. Jamie had been fully aware of Kelsey's disappointment with not being able to get the answers she wanted regarding her dad and had considered on several occasions telling her what she knew, which wasn't much. Since she had professionally made an agreement with Kelsey's loved ones, she did not want to go back on her word.

This period had taken its toll on Jamie as well. With over twenty years of friendship, and Kelsey unable to respond to her as she used to, Jamie felt alone and confused. It was a catch 22. It would be so easy to tell Kelsey everything she knew just as it had been easy for her to let Kelsey work through this situation for herself. Telling Kelsey her past would solve all of Jamie's problems as she would possibly gain an ally. However, the domino effect with her mother and husband's relationships could prove to be too damaging for her godchildren, and she refused to risk their happiness. Jamie's last hope was to try and get Kelsey to open up, and she needed the family's support.

Even though Jamie called a family meeting at her office for later this evening, she had been on pins and needles all day. She would have to try and restore order in the midst of Mom's dramatic chaos and console Gregory all the while holding it together for herself. How simple life would have been if Kelsey hadn't had the accident. How simple life would be if Kelsey would realize how much Jamie loved her and needed her friendship. Nothing has been able to fill the void since the loss of Jamie's closest confidant. A social life for Jamie has been all but lost except for her weekly meetings at the local shelter. There Jamie consoles battered women, and even though she had met several women that she had grown fond of over the last two years, nothing had compared to the relationship she had with Kelsey.

There are no current prospects for romance, so most nights after work, Jamie heads home to her condo and her Yorkshire terrier, Miro. As an avid reader, Jamie spends most of her time researching Kelsey's condition and new techniques that will assist her friend. Even though a number of colleagues had suggested hypnosis, Jamie had feared that without being able to control a specific memory, Kelsey could regurgitate any number of scarring memories and cause herself to spiral out of control if she were inundated with too much too soon. However, as Kelsey's therapist, the session would have to be up to Gregory, a suggestion she planned to introduce at tonight's meeting.

"I called this meeting so that we could openly talk about Kelsey and her current condition. I've noticed that Kelsey's demeanor has changed in our sessions; she is barely opening up to me like she used to.

Kelsey has become extremely pessimistic, and her attitude will grow darker if we don't intervene and come up with a plan to help her.

I need both of you to be extremely honest with me tonight as holding back any information will only be to Kelsey's detriment, and I know we all have the best intentions for her," Jamie said confidently. She could see the concern on Gregory's face, but Mom looked petrified.

"I need all of us to put aside whatever differences we may personally have with Kelsey and focus on what is going to help her in the long run," she continued. "I'm asking that we open up to each other and try to figure out a way to assist Kelsey out of the slump and help her move forward or we could lose her altogether," they both listened intently.

"Jamie, thank you for all of your hard work these last few years," Gregory stated. "Personally, I'm at my wits end with Kelsey. She has grown hostile towards me and I am growing extremely tired of the abuse."

"What abuse?" Jamie asked.

"Lately, she belittles me in front of the kids a lot. Nothing is ever good enough, and I can't seem to do anything right for her."

"Heck, she sounds normal to me," Mom threw in.

"Mom, this is different. I mean, she has become nasty, and she looks at me as if she hates me. I feel as if she blames me for something, but she won't come out and say what the problem is. It's unnerving. She snaps at me a lot and touching my own wife is out of the question. She's just selfish."

"Gregory, I'm sorry to hear that she's this way towards you. Kelsey mentioned in several sessions that she had asked you to do something for her and that you had not completed it. Do you think this is what has agitated her?" Jamie questioned him looking directly into his eyes trying to let him know that she knew what that something was, so he didn't need to go into any detail in front of Mom. She knew he would pick up on her clues regarding finding out information regarding her father.

Gregory looked pensive, then responded. "What does she want from me?" he yelled. "That's all she talks about. She's obsessed. Why can't she just move on?" Gregory was stressed.

"Talks about what?" Mom asked feeling out of the loop.

"Information about her stupid father, Kerri-Claire!" Gregory yelled at his mother-in-law out of frustration. "Why can't you just tell her what happened so we can all move on with our lives? I've been holding up my end of the bargain by not speaking about things that are outside of our marriage, as we all swore to do, but this is ridiculous!"

"Gregory, calm down. Yelling at her isn't going to make things any easier," Jamie intervened.

"It's my business, and if I don't want to open up a can of worms, then you will have to respect my decision," Mom countered.

"Don't you see you are making the lives of your grandbabies, mine, and Kelsey's a living hell? Don't you care? What is the big deal? So, you weren't married to Kelsey's father, no one cares nowadays! You would think you would be considerate of those who have to live with your daughter on a daily basis!" He was fuming as Mom began to cry. Jamie knew she should have stopped him, but it was good for him to get this stuff off of his chest. Besides, Jamie never knew the whole story and hoped Mom might spill the beans.

"You're cruel, Gregory! I had just recently confided that information to you in trust! How dare you throw that up in my face now! You only care about your selfish needs and wants and have no regard for others," she yelled back as she reached for a couple of tissues from the box on Jamie's desk.

"What are you talking about? My marriage is falling apart, I'm considering leaving your daughter for someone who can truly appreciate me, and the one thing that can at least give her a little peace you refuse to give to her. No one is judging you, Kerri-Claire; no one blames you for a relationship gone awry. I am trying to hold onto my wits and my marriage together, and if something doesn't change soon—I'M OUT!"

"Mom, what happened was so long ago. No one will judge you if that is what you fear," Jamie offered as she handed Mom more tissues.

"It's no one's business! It's no one's business but my own!"

"Kerri-Claire, you are so wrong," Gregory concluded before getting up to go to the bathroom.

"Mom, you have to free yourself of the pain that you have obviously bottled up inside for years. Tell your story and release the pain. Mom, it's time to be free," Jamie said calmly while wrapping her arms around her best friend's mother trying to offer some comfort.

Mom knew she was right, took a deep breath and began to confess. Though she had not uttered the full ordeal in years, Mom could see the events unfold as if it were yesterday.

Kerri-Claire grew up in the church with strict parents, so she wasn't able to date during high school. "Show me dating in the Bible, and you can go on one," her loving but firm father would say often. His stern parenting style prevented her from accepting the numerous dates with boys who constantly asked her. Though she was tempted by her friends to sneak out on an occasion or two, Kerri-Claire was too petrified at the idea of getting caught. Good girls just didn't do that.

She had always known that she was a pretty, young woman. She would constantly get whistles from her classmates when she walked down the street and a few older men. Kerri-Claire had learned how to work her womanly curves on her young body by dancing a couple of times in her mirror with few friends. She had learned to subtly switch her wide hips, flip her long flowing mane, and slightly jiggle her firm bosom under her tight sweaters. She would even get a kick out of flirting with the bag boy or gas attendant, practicing for when she would seduce her husband. Though she loved being a tease, she was a fraud. Kerri-Claire believed that saving herself for her wedding night was the best way to honor God and her father.

Kerri-Claire had never seen a man as handsome as Junior Watkins in her life. He was tall, with a muscular but slim build, his dimples, and curly sandy brown hair made her swoon. His high forehead was a sign of strength,, and his long, dreamy lashes lightly brushed up against his spectacles as his grayish-green eyes appeared to look right through you. He dressed impeccably well and all the girls on Kerri-Claire's college campus had a crush on him. His warm smile enhanced his cleft chin which sent Kerri-Claire's heart into orbit. Even in her dreams, it was hard for Kerri-Claire to think that Junior would be interested in her. So, when Junior asked her to the movies one day in her freshman year of college, she suspiciously thought her dad had paid him to test her while she was living in the dorms. It took weeks of persistence to finally convince her that Junior was truly was interested.

Junior and Kerri-Claire quickly became an item and known on the small college campus as the couple that was inseparable. It was not surprising that at the beginning of her junior year, Junior Watkins asked her to be his wife. Even her father was proud of the humble man who was entering his first year of med school. They were the perfect couple—she was studying to be a nurse and he was going to be the first doctor in his family. Both parents were proud of their children, often had dinners at each other's homes, and even took trips together. The Watkins even joined Kerri-Claire's father's church, and Junior attended it regularly with Kelsey. On several occasions, Kerri-Claire's father called Junior "son" as if he were preparing himself for the many years they would spend together.

Everything had been planned. They would marry the summer after Kerri-Claire had graduated, have three kids, and would save up enough money for Junior to open his own practice. Kerri-Claire would assist him by running the front office. She could still see the gold-plated door sign, *Watkins Medical Center,* she had purchased as a gift for Junior that Christmas. Everything was perfect…until the night of the winter social. Junior and Kerri-Claire had gotten dressed to the nines as usual and were headed to the event. Junior had suggested that they park for a little bit because they both had been so busy with schoolwork and tests that they had not seen each other regularly for weeks. As Junior pulled over in the park, even though there was no snow on the ground, the night air was chilly.

"Junior, you're crazy! We'll freeze out here," Kerri-Claire protested.

"Awww, that's why I have you, baby. You're supposed to keep me warm," he whispered soothingly in her ear. Kerri-Claire couldn't resist his charm, and before she knew it, her 20-year-old body had experienced a pleasure she had never known. Everything she had promised herself and her father had gone up in smoke, and she didn't care. What was the big deal? She was going to be Mrs. Junior Watkins in eighteen months anyway. She had a ½ carat diamond engagement ring on her finger to prove it. Now she was his, body and soul, and they made it to the dance that night.

Many days afterward, Kerri-Claire had replayed that wintry night in her mind over and over and decided to never regret it—until she missed her next menstrual cycle.

"What do you mean you're pregnant? What kind of nursing student are you who isn't bright enough to be on the pill?" Junior shouted at her when she told him that the doctor confirmed her pregnancy.

"Why would I need to be on the pill if I were waiting to have sex our wedding night? There was no need to be on the pill! What about you, Dr. Watkins? You're the one that forgot to bring a rubber?" Kerri-Claire retorted. It went on like that over an hour, each blaming the other for their mistake—both terrified that they had ruined their careers. Kerri-Claire cried so hard when Junior took her to a clinic and suggested that she get rid of it.

"Have you lost your mind? I can't kill my baby!" she objected. "So, you would rather your father kill me instead? You would rather my career go down the drain? How am I gonna support you, a baby, and medical school?"

"Junior, it won't be that bad. I know it's not what we planned, but we can make it. Our folks can help out. I'll finish up school at nights, and you can, too," she optimistically suggested, but he wouldn't hear of it.

"Kerri-Claire, you have two choices; either get rid of it, or you're on your own." With that, he turned and walked down the street, leaving Kerri-Claire standing in front of the doctor's office.

What Kerri-Claire thought was the most painful thing she had to deal with was nothing in comparison to having to admit to her dad that his precious little girl was pregnant. Disgusted and shamed, James C. Rollins didn't speak to his own flesh and blood for a month. He was embarrassed and hurt that his daughter had made such a poor choice—she had been raised better than that. But he was more ashamed that the young man he had once called son had abandoned her. It was truly the grace of God that kept James from killing the boy, but to make matters worse, The Watkins had rallied around their son, blaming Kerri-Claire for the situation. What used to be a loving friendship between soon-to-be extended family members quickly became The Hatfield's and The McCoy's.

Pregnant and on the verge of a nervous breakdown, at the suggestion of her mother, Kerri-Claire dropped out of college, climbed on a bus, and headed down to New Orleans to stay with her favorite cousin, Pauline. It was there that Kerri-Claire concocted what would be the love affair of Jay Smith. It was there that she changed her name from Rollins to Smith and vowed to wipe the memory of Junior Watkins from her memory forever. It was there, as she held her new little baby girl, that she vowed never to tell her how unscrupulous her real father was. It was at that moment that she vowed to never trust a man again.

The three of them just sat in silence for a while trying to absorb what Mom had just confessed. Mom had to admit that unloading her secret did make her feel twenty pounds lighter.

"I'm sorry about what happened to you, Mom, and forgive me for getting upset," Gregory humbly stated. "But, Mom, times have changed. There are movies on *Lifetime* that are more jarring than what you just admitted."

"I agree. I don't know what you've been so terrified of all of these years," added Jamie.

"I don't care if you both don't get it. I personally didn't want to relive that horrible experience ever again. Not to mention, you and I both know that Kelsey is so strong-willed that she'd look up Junior just to give him a piece of her mind. I don't ever want to see or have to hear about him ever again."

I returned home late from my retreat. At the suggestion of my Mentor, I had taken another day to truly unwind. I was so distraught at the thought of wanting to kill myself that I could no longer stay in my luxury penthouse suite and checked into another hotel. It wasn't until after I got off the phone with my Mentor that I realized that I had planned to go to Eden Roc to eradicate myself all along. It had not occurred to me during my stay, and come to think of it, when I was packing for my trip, that I had contemplated doing such a thing. What made it even more hurtful was accepting the fact that I am not on any medication, so my perfectly planned finale was the work of a sober mind.

Even though my flight landed at 9 p.m., I got in my car and drove down to the Jersey Shore so that I could think. To be completely truthful, I needed some time to prepare myself to return to the chaos. I had to get a hold of my facilities so that I could pull myself out of whatever phase I was going through.

The house was so quiet when I walked up the stairs. I was startled to see that at 1 a.m., my children weren't in their beds. Both bedrooms were perfectly tidy with all of their toys neatly put in their proper place and beds made. I did appreciate that. I was overwhelmed when I opened the door to my bedroom suite and found my kids snuggled in the bed with their father. My beautiful babies were mirror images of my husband, and they looked like one person in different stages of his life. What a sight it was to see this grown man embracing his sons, and their hands clutching him for dear life. It was a tender moment—one I pray I will never forget. *This is what you have to live for, Kelsey, even if it is not always perfect.* I dropped to my knees and thanked God that I didn't let my selfishness take me away from such a sweet moment like this. I will have to always remember this moment especially when I feel low.

Chapter Twenty-One

Am I Crazy?

As I closed my tear-stained eyes, my exhausted, and wilted body was happy to be lying on something soft. It was great to smell the familiar scent of home, and it was even greater to wake up in the woods again. I saw my two friends sitting across from, me and I began to tell them about my birthday weekend.

"Kelsey, you would kill yourself because you never met a man?" Isabel wasted no time slamming me.

"It wasn't over a man…the fact is I'm tired!"

"Tired of what?" she continued to grill me.

"Of the not knowing."

"The not knowing is half the fun," Moriah chimed in.

"Is it fun not to remember things that are crucially important to you?" I lost my temper with both of them. "You don't know what it's like to be near a man that when he reaches out to you, your entire body grows stiff with anticipation knowing his clammy hands are gonna feel grotesque. You don't know what it's like to know that the woman who had you would rather lie to you than tell you what you have a right to know so that you can be healed. Why does she pretend to want me to get better if she is part of the problem? Do you have any idea what it feels like to know that a woman would be satisfied with spending two or three times a week with me purging just to be able to call me her best friend? Instead of going out and creating a life of her own, she is content with being with a person who not only can't remember her but only considers her as close as a therapist? I have a husband that has to live like a monk because I

141

can't even imagine having sex with him, a best friend that is a spinster in her early thirties, and a mother who I believe hates me." I let it all hang out and it felt good to get these things off my chest. Dr. Jamie would have been proud.

They both stared at me as if I hadn't said a thing. Moriah had the sweetest and warm look on her face, but Isabel appeared to have a slight smirk on hers. With one eyebrow up, Isabel spoke after a moment or two.

"Kelsey, why are you so pessimistic?"

"I'm not pessimistic, I'm a realist," I answered.

"Same thing," Moriah chimed in.

"Darling, there are so many things that you can't see, but are so clear to me. Did it ever occur to you that maybe your father was removed from your life at such an early age because he had nothing to contribute to it? Did you ever think the reason you have no feelings towards that man you chose to be with for the rest of your life is because you haven't cultivated true intimacy in your own life?" Isabel stated.

I was dumbfounded. It was the first time Isabel sounded nurturing. Moriah spoke up, "Did you consider that what happened long ago between your mother and father may be an excruciating memory for her? Why haven't you considered that Jamie loves you so much that living the way she does hasn't been a second thought for her because she understands the concept of sacrifice?"

"If the tables were turned, could you have done the same for Jamie? It's time you take a moment and evaluate all sides of this situation before you react or make snap decisions," Isabel took up the slack.

By the time they finished their comments, I had my head in my hands, and tears were seeping through my tightly closed fingers.

For the next couple of days, I walked on eggshells trying to keep a low profile until I had a moment to sort things out. I was silent most of the time, and Gregory was quick to make sure that everything was all right.

"I'm fine," I replied, trying to sound as positive as I could hoping that he didn't think I was mad at him. The truth was, I wasn't mad…I just needed to be silent for a while. So, I stayed in my room, read, and watched a little television. My mother had the kids, so it was pretty quiet around our home.

I limited the time I slept so that I would not have to face my interrogators. As much as I knew they were interjecting sound advice, it felt more like they were rendering judgment, and I was not up for that again.

When I spoke to my Mentor, I wasn't able to fully articulate the intensity of Isabel and Moriah's comments, but the message was clear. I had to reevaluate my life and relationships. I had to put the mirror up in front of my face and take a good look at what may be my warped way of thinking.

This was the first time that I could remember in years that my Mentor didn't say anything. I mean, he didn't even respond with a grunt or a sigh. It was as if I were talking into a dead phone. I knew he was there by his faint and steady breathing. Then it occurred to me that he may have fallen asleep.

Chapter Twenty-Two

From Bad to Worse

"How much longer do I have to put up with this?" Gregory pleaded. "It doesn't look like she's even trying anymore. She's becoming more distant and colder. Why am I staying in a situation that isn't healthy for our kids or me?"

It was the first time that I heard Gregory speak out about my selfishness. It was 3:26 a.m., I had stumbled out of bed to use the bathroom, and there he was, crouched down by the sink, pouring out his heart. Since losing my memory, everything was about me and it didn't matter what it was doing to him. My concern was always regarding the kids but never Gregory. I was so busy pouring salt on my own wounds, basking in my problems, that I hadn't thought twice about how hard it must be to care for someone in my condition. I'm sure other men in his situation would have thrown me in an insane asylum and had another woman in two days as good-looking as Gregory is.

"What did I do to deserve this? I know I've never been perfect, but have I been so bad in my life that I deserve to spend the rest of my life tied to a woman that can't remember how much she loved me and our children? Is it fair that I'm mistreated and talked down to like I'm a child! I'm holding on by a thread, and I feel like you aren't giving me the support I need," he vented.

Boy, he was pissed. Did I say something that ticked him off today? Think, Kelsey, think. I can't recall ever hearing him like this in the last three years. He sounded mad, but even more so, broken.

Then I heard him say my Mentor's name and I lost it. How dare Gregory go behind my back and discuss his problems with MY MENTOR? I stormed in.

"What do you think you're doing?" I questioned.

"Kelsey, I'm not in the mood tonight. I need some time to myself; please leave, okay?"

"Are you going to answer my question?" "What are you talking about?"

"To whom were you talking to just now?"

He angrily pushed pass me, tossing the phone onto the bed. "I told you I don't want to discuss it right now. Get off my back and leave me alone!"

"How dare you talk to me like that?"

Spinning around with his hands high as if he were going to wring my neck, he yelled, "What? The way you talk to me out the side of your neck, you are kidding, right? Man, you're lucky I don't hit women!"

"Oh, so now you're gonna hit me? You sneak behind my back, talk to my friend, and now you're threatening me?"

"Stop babbling. What friend was I talking to?"

"Don't deny it, I heard you talking to my Mentor about me. How dare you! Don't you ever do that again!" Now I was pissed.

"Look you crazy..." he stopped as soon as he said it. "I'm sorry, I didn't mean to call you that."

"DON'T YOU EVER CALL ME CRAZY! I am mentally challenged due to a traumatic blow to the head! FOR ALL I KNOW YOU'RE THE ONE WHO PROBABLY DROVE ME CRAZY!" I screamed at the top of my lungs.

"NO, YOU WERE THERE LONG BEFORE I CAME AROUND!"

He was getting venomous. "I will talk to whomever I please, and if I need to discuss how I feel with someone who understands, I will. Got it! You should be happy I'm trying to figure out how to stay in this ridiculous marriage." Tears were streaming down his cheek. He was hurting, and here I was jealous that he wanted to purge whatever bad feelings he was having to the one person I trusted the most.

"Everything is about you and how you are feeling. What about the rest of us who are stuck in this hell with you? Do you think about how your continued selfishness will affect the kids? You're selfish, Kelsey, hard as nails, and just plain selfish. I can't do this. I don't want this anymore. I've tried for too long, you're regressing, and you don't even care." He was full-fledge sobbing now.

"What do you mean I don't care? I'm trying and going as fast as I can, but apparently you just can't turn memories off and on."

"Kelsey, it's been three long years. Baby, don't you feel anything for me? Putting your situation aside, can't you see that I love you? Don't you want to see that I love you?" he questioned, putting his arms around me.

Pulling away, I replied, "Why are you asking me all of these questions? I love you as much as I can for right now. It just would be helpful if I could remember who you really are or were back when we first met."

"Why? What does it matter now?"

"Why? Because I need to know that I didn't make a mistake…I," There it was. It just came out, but it was the truth. He looked at me for a long time before shaking his head and walking out of the bedroom. "Gregory, what I meant to say is that I want to be perfect for you and the kids, and I don't think I can if I can't recall our history."

"No, Kelsey, you just want to be perfect." His words were so cold that I just stood staring at him. He was right, I did. I was waiting to perfectly regain all of my memories so I could just pick up the pieces and move forward from there.

"Kelsey, the truth is that our past wasn't perfect, and neither was I. Neither were you, for that matter, or the way we lived. But it was a good life that was beginning to get better until you had your episode. The past isn't who we are now because it is over. It's up to us to get over it."

146

"How can I get over something I don't remember?"

"Maybe it's you who is choosing not to remember the past, and now you're running from the future at the same time." With that he continued down the hallway, walked down the stairs, and walked out of the house.

I couldn't wait until my appointment with Dr. Jamie the next day. I needed a voice of reason that could understand how I was feeling and make me understand why I got so angry last night when I heard Gregory talking to my Mentor. I pulled up into the parking lot, parked, and I rushed to catch an elevator. As I tried to make the doors, I could see some young punks looking carelessly at me as the doors almost slammed dead in my face. I gave the door a karate whack as if to say, "you better not close on me," and watched the doors politely open so I could stroll in.

"Sorry, I didn't see you coming," said an elderly lady who was standing by the elevator buttons—I believed her.

"No worries, you know how it is, ma'am, some people were had, and others raised!" I proclaimed as I flipped my long hair over my shoulders and tossed it into one of the young men's face. As I stepped out of the elevator onto the 16th floor, the young man whose face I hit with my hair grumbled something under his breath to his friend and they both snickered.

"What?" I questioned as I turned around to face him.

"I said it figures," he boldly replied.

"What figures?"

"The "crazy lady" would be getting off on the crazy people's floor," he jabbed as the doors shut. I stared at the closed door, and my eyes darted to the right where a sign read *Clay Memorial Psychiatric Floor*. That was the second time within 24 hours I was called "crazy."

"Some people have such limited vocabulary!" I quipped. I stormed into Dr. Jamie's office at the hospital and was greeted by her assistant.

"Good afternoon, Mrs. Smith-Pritchard. You're here early today."

"When is Dr. Jamie moving out of this hospital and into a *real* office?" I blurted. "I am so tired of people looking at me as if I'm one of these screwy people in this ward." It was the first time I had ever really acknowledged that I had been going to a hospital for my visits. Or maybe it was the first time I even noticed.

"You look nice today, Mrs. Smith-Pritchard. Going somewhere special after your appointment?" she asked disregarding my question.

"Are you implying that I don't usually look nice?" Squirm out of that one.

"Oh no, not at all Mrs. Smith-Pritchard, it's just you look especially nice today in your business suit," she replied backpedaling.

"I got a closet full of suits just like this one. There was a time when I wore suits like this every day. I'm getting tired of waiting for you to answer my question. When will your office be moving?"

Answer me!

"We're moving? Nobody told me?" Dr. Jamie asked. She startled me. I spun around to look her in the face.

"Are you planning on moving out of here? I just had someone call me crazy as I got off the elevator."

"Come in, Kelsey."

"Ever thought about it?"

"What?"

"Moving into a real office space."

"Kelsey, I've always had my own office space. When you had your episode, I moved in here so I could closely monitor you," she finished.

"Well, that's a lot to dump on someone. Why did you do that?"

"Well, my lease was almost over, and it was no big deal."

"What do you mean no big deal? You altered your entire practice to be closer to me, and this is the first time to hear of it. I feel like an idiot!"

"Why does that make you feel like an idiot?"

"Who am I that you have to do that for? What about your other patients?"

"Kelsey, my other patients weren't my best friend for over two decades!"

My eyes began welling up. "Why is everyone making me feel like I was the cause for his or her decisions? First my mom, then Gregory, and now you—who am I to have that much control over people?"

Dr. Jamie had a peculiar look on her face as if she were trying to control her temper, and calmly asked, "What's bothering you? Did something happen? I can't speak for the others, but I made my decision because I care deeply about you and your condition. I'm actually happy with my current arrangement. I'm on the Board of Directors here at the hospital, and they are constantly referring new patients to me. My practice has doubled since I made the decision to come here. It has been a win-win situation for all concerned."

She handed me a tissue, and I tried to tell her about last night without fully breaking down. Dr. Jamie listened carefully, studying me.

"What's the matter?" I asked after I was finished unloading my spat with Gregory.

"It puzzles me that you really don't know how much people care for you." she replied.

"What do you mean?"

"You have no idea that you are loved, and people are trying to do whatever it takes to help you through this period, no matter what the cost."

"So, you're saying I'm a bad person because everyone is doing so much for me and I'm too ungrateful to realize it?"

"YEAH!" She yelled at me so quickly it startled me. Now she was pissed with me.

"Kelsey, it is not you against the world. You happen to be blessed with people, imperfect people mind you, who want you to be happy and completely well. But maybe that is not possible. In some way, you believe everyone thinks you are perfect and that you have to function that way."

I began to cry, but she didn't let up.

"Kelsey, you need to get over yourself and understand that we all fall short of perfection, but we are all working with what we have. Nobody is perfect. You've got a perfectly good man who has exhausted everything that he is and knows how to be there for you, and you still look at him as if he can't get it right. I've known you for too long, and I know that I've had a hand in letting you become the monster you are today, both selfish and manipulative. You lived your entire life behind a mask trying to conceal your pain, and life has flipped flopped, and you are actually living as the mean-spirited person you really are through your sulking. Despite of all of that, Gregory *still* wants and loves you and wants to make your marriage work and stand by your side."

Her words kept pounding against my head until I broke down sobbing uncontrollably. I couldn't breathe, but mercilessly she continued.

"Do you know how many women would kill to have a man like Gregory? One who respects them and loves them unconditionally? Do you know how many people I counsel? You better believe that numerous men in Gregory's position would have never even claimed you after your accident! Still, this man tries, Kelsey! He really tries! Who are you to break his spirit and efforts of trying to love you? Who are you that you can abuse this man's feelings? Gregory called it right. You think you'll find perfection at the end of the road, but your road should not lead to a dead end! You should be looking to get to the right intersection. An intersection that will lead you somewhere other than Fantasyville! You should want to let go of the past; your mind does!"

This was not the Dr. Jamie I knew. This was just plain Jamie. She got so far up my butt, I didn't know what to say or do next. I just kept trying to breathe. I began gasping for air.

"Cut the dramatics, Kelsey; you can breathe just fine. You got yourself into this mess. And another thing, don't you EVER compare me to your mother! I don't deserve that. I've sacrificed over the past three years to be there for you hoping you will remember me, too, but I've come to the conclusion you don't want my friendship. I'm just 'Dr. Jamie' to you now that you got your two *new* friends. Personally, I don't think you can handle real friendships anymore."

"What are you talking about? Aren't you my friend?"

"What kind of friend am I to you if, after all we've been through, you choose to run to figments of your imagination instead of confiding in me?" So, there it was.

"Jamie, are you jealous of my friendship with Isabel and Moriah?" I asked with both eyes swelling up from my stinging tears.

"What friendship? If you want to find comfort in having multiple conversations with yourself while you are sleeping, that's your choice. Call it delusional, or whatever you like, just don't call that friendship! You can't remember what a true friendship is, so don't use the word!"

Sitting inside my car, I cried and cried. To tell you the truth, it felt good. It was out in the open. For so long, the people who loved me the most have had to bottle up their emotions for the sake of my sanity, and it has been wearing thin on them. I had no idea that my excitement for my conversations with Isabel and Moriah had hurt Jamie, or that my interaction with them had pushed us apart. I just looked at Jamie as a doctor but, in fact, she never stopped looking at me as her friend. I felt so ashamed of that moment. Two people who I know loved me were hurting now but loved me enough to tell me the truth. Jamie was right. Without remembering a thing from my past, I knew she wouldn't abuse her authority as a doctor or talk to me in that manner unless it was love. Jamie wouldn't lie to me about who I was and who I've become. I knew love wouldn't allow her to do that.

Chapter Twenty-Three

Where Have You Been?

"Where have you been?"

"Around, I've just been taking a break to see if I can clear my head. It's been a rough couple of days," I responded trying to sound hopeful, but I felt hopeless. I hadn't spoken much since my conversations with Gregory and Jamie, not even to my Mentor. I felt depressed yesterday, so I stayed in bed all day, and even missed an appointment with Dr. Jamie. It was the first time in three years that I'd ever missed an appointment with her. I rescheduled it for next week. I'm sure the break did both of us good. Gregory's traveling, so my mom took the kids to give me a little break.

"You sound troubled; do you want to talk about it?" his voice was so calming, and before I knew it, I regurgitated the episodes to him between sobs. He listened intently, and his comments were laced with love.

"Maybe you are being too hard on yourself?" he responded after I unloaded the mess. "It's good that you are sensitive and reflective but beating yourself up as if you are incapable of doing anything right won't solve anything," he finished. He was right.

"So, what do I do now that I know that everybody hates me?" I pouted.

"Is that what you are taking from all of this?"

"Well, no, but I feel so stupid, I don't know what to say." It was true I felt as if I had been tippy-toeing around everyone.

"Try apologizing for starters. Then let them apologize to you," he said bluntly.

"Why are they apologizing? They're right. I have been selfish and self-centered. I do take everybody's feelings for granted. I'm everything they said, and much more."

"All of that may be true. I am not excusing your behavior, but it doesn't mean that they could not have tried to restrain themselves," he stated.

"But it was me who backed them into a corner. I have a way of pushing people over the edge, and when they blow their stack, their reaction is more out of self-defense than control. It's true. I'm a manipulator."

"Was it self-defense or lack of communication on their part?"

"What are you talking about? I do not understand you." I was puzzled. For the first time I owned up to my faults, and he was finding fault with Gregory and Jamie. "I know exactly what I did and I'm tired of glossing over the facts. I have been inconsiderate of other's feelings and so wrapped up in my own issues that I never bothered to ask them about themselves."

"Kelsey, now you are going from being a manipulator to a martyr. Communication is a two-way street. How could you have known that Dr. Jamie was feeling uneasy about her role in your life if she only presented herself to you as your doctor? Not once has she tried to extend herself to you after hours or outside of the office except when she was your mediator around friends. Never do you spend one-on-one time together so that you can bond. You both spend all of your time interacting with each other as doctor and patient instead of best friends. This type of interaction puts her in the position of your savior instead of your friend. Have you two ever had a regular conversation without her trying to analyze you?"

"Well, no, not that I can remember," I answered honestly.

"It seems to me she was the one playing the manipulator trying to fill a dominant role in your life. Due to your strong personality, is it possible that during the twenty-plus years you've shared as friends, you played the dominant role in the relationship? Since your episode, she's been able to ride in on her white horse and save you."

Could that be true? "I hadn't thought about it like that before," I answered, looking for more wisdom.

"Kelsey, you have become a daughter to me, and there is nothing I want more for you than to be happy and move forward with your life. Don't get me wrong, you have good people around you. They love and care for you very much, but sometimes even loving someone too much can cause people to make the wrong choices. Understand? Gregory wants you to be healthy and happy and is ready to move forward with your lives, but he has not been helpful by not communicating regarding his own feelings and his own mistakes with you.

He's scared and has a lot to learn about communication. During the last three years, he had to grow up. Before, you were a strong presence in the marriage, and you assumed the leadership role because you are a born leader. Instead of admitting he doesn't know what he is doing, like most men, he internalizes everything, and he tries to mask his feelings of fear. Kelsey, I've noticed that you have a strong spirit that can instinctively see through a person's BS, shooting them down in an effort to try to rid yourself of any confusion.

Your biggest problem isn't just being insensitive to others but that you are extremely impatient."

He was dead on. I have found in the last three years that I have a low tolerance for the bull. "I just have no patience."

"Patience is a virtue," he quoted sweetly.

"How can I become more patient?" I asked really wanting to know.

"First, you have to want to be patient. Then realize that others have been extremely patient with you. Secondly, you need to learn how to extend grace to others and yourself. Thirdly, you need to learn to be fluid. Being so mechanical and rigid is not good. You have two beautiful boys you need to raise which will require a lot of patience and grace."

"Boy don't I know it!" I quipped. "Sometimes I look into their little faces and wonder what was I thinking about wanting to become a mother." It just came out. It was as if my Mentor used some secret Jedi mind trick. I couldn't believe I said it so plainly, and I know I must have sounded like a terrible mother.

"Have you ever thought that maybe they chose you, and you simply accepted the gift of their love?" he asked just as simple as that.

"Now you are making me feel horrible. I look at their baby pictures, and even though I look happy, everything feels fake."

"Fake?"

"Yeah, something is clearly missing in me. They look like they are my possessions. I look at the house, my business, my husband, and all that we have acquired, but something must have been missing for me to snap the way I did. I don't know it's just…well, I don't know."

"What, child, what?" he pushed.

"Well, to be truthful, it seems as if I was accumulating all of these things to appear successful, but I was very unhappy," I answered.

"Sometimes women want to have children more than wanting to be mothers. Do you think it was unhappiness or emptiness?" he questioned me as if he already knew the answer.

"Why do you say it like that?"

"It's just that I have found over the years that hoarding is a sign of emptiness." I could almost see him looking at me through the phone.

"I don't know. I'm gonna have to think on that one," I truthfully replied.

"Do that and let me know what you come up with. By the way, why don't you want Gregory to talk to me?"

"I guess I felt a little jealous. I've always thought of you as my friend, and it was nice to have you all to myself," I admitted honestly.

"Sweetie, I'm everyone's friend."

Chapter Twenty-Four

Give It to Me Straight, Jamie

Even though I missed an appointment last week, both Jamie and I acted as if our last conversation never happened. When I walked into her office, we said our hellos and jumped right into the session. "I can't take this anymore. Jamie, you're gonna have to give me some answers."

"What is it that you want to know, Kelsey?" she questioned.

"I want to know everything. I want to know why this happened to me, who I am, and have every question answered. You've been my best friend for years. I don't understand why you just can't fill in the blanks for me."

"Kelsey, I strongly recommend that you let your mind take its time to heal."

"I've done that for over three years. My husband is ready to leave me. He blames me for not getting better fast enough, and he keeps accusing me of not trying. I swear, I am, but this isn't easy. I can't just turn my feelings or my memories on and off just because he wants me to. Why won't you help me?" I begged.

"I am trying to help you the best way I professionally can. Kelsey, I don't think Gregory wants you to turn your emotions or your feelings towards him on or off, I think he wants you to simply respond to him."

"How do you respond to something you can't remember? How do you respond to someone you don't know? Something is seriously off, and I can't put my finger on it."

"Wait a minute. Are you telling me that you have been living with Gregory for the last three and a half years and you feel nothing

156

towards him? You don't look at him and see that he's a handsome man?"

"Well, I don't know. No, I guess," I answered honestly. "Kelsey, how is that possible?"

"I don't know!" I was telling the truth. "I can't explain how I feel or don't feel for Gregory, or why there's no emotion towards him right now."

"Do you want to feel anything for Gregory?"

"I don't know," I repeated.

"Then maybe you should let him go. After all this time, it would be completely selfish if you stayed with this man or try to make him stay if he doesn't want to. Maybe it's time to just let things go. You've done your best, right?" she probed.

"Honestly, I don't know. I believe I've done as much as I can. I've had to discover so many things in the last three years while trying to remember myself at the same time. I know I can't continue being with someone who deserves more, and I just don't know when or if I can give him what he wants. At the same time, I don't think it's fair that he gets a pass and just leaves me without giving me adequate time to work things out."

"So, you don't think that over three years is adequate time?"

"Not when you've made a pact that is bound by 'til death do you part!'"

"When is the last time you guys made love?"

"We haven't. There have been a few times that the idea of sex was tempting, but then when I get around Gregory, I get distracted with something, and the feeling goes away. I guess with all that is going on, I don't have a sexual appetite."

She just looked at me for a while with her mouth half-open. "You're telling me that every night you lay next to Gregory—with his muscular body—and you have no desire for him at ALL?" She said it so loud, I almost felt as if I had done something wrong.

"I just don't want to complicate things by having sex with him and send him the wrong signals."

"Kelsey, this isn't someone you are dating. Signals don't exist anymore. This is your husband; remember, 'til death do you part.' Whether you can remember it or not, your body no longer belongs to you anymore…it's his now."

"That's what I don't think anyone understands; he's like a stranger to me. I have no recollection of any memory or any time with this man. I can't remember anything, Jamie, I mean nothing!" I yelled back at her trying to prove my point.

"I know you can't remember anything, but it's been three and a half years. What is remembering going to do for you at this point?"

"As I said before, it's gonna give me closure. A chance for me to believe my brain's capable of functioning correctly again. It's going to give me a sense of who I am or was so and that I can move forward without it shutting down again."

"But your brain shut down due to a severe head injury. Remember?" For the first time in three and a half years, she stopped the tape recorder that was recording our session. She stared out of the window that was beside her desk and kept turning the pen in her hand. As she turned her attention towards me, she tapped the pen on her upper lip, took a deep breath and began to speak.

"Off the record, I can't understand what you're going through. As much as I want to, there is no way that I can logically comprehend what your life has been like since your accident. You have always been like a sister to me, and I love you with all my heart, but I really think it's time that you stop trying to remember the past and get on with your life. I am giving you this advice as your best friend, as your sister, and someone who loves you very much. It's not healthy for you to continue living this way. It's not good for my godchildren or for the man I've always considered as my brother for almost eight years. I think it's time you really look at how you would live your life without Gregory."

"So, you're saying I should give up?" I asked hurt. I had not even considered life without Gregory. "I thought marriage was supposed to be unconditional. Where does it say in our vows that having amnesia gives my husband the right to leave me?"

"I'm saying it appears that you have given up because you refuse to pick up the pieces and move forward. Remember last year when I asked you what would you do if you never remembered anything from the past? Have you made any plans if that becomes your reality?"

"I still have never considered that as an option. I guess I have always remained optimistic that my memory would come back, and I would be safe in knowing that this drama has ended, then I could move forward. I would remember the truth about my dad, I would remember what is really going on with my mother, and I would be able to share the memories of our friendship. I want to know for myself that Gregory was the love of my life. I want to be able to remember that my child loves peanut butter, that he can't stand jelly, and why. I'm tired of feeling empty." I paused for a moment fighting back the tears.

"I'm tired of feeling like a mental case. Did it ever occur to anyone that maybe all those things would be important to me?" I asked.

"Why do you think it's hopeless?"

"I'm tired of having to rely on what people refuse to tell me. I want to know for myself. I cannot just say, 'Okay, dear. I'll stop hoping that I can remember how much I love you, or how your touch used to feel. What if this situation happened to you, Dr. Jamie?"

"Kelsey, I've just told you I can't even imagine what you're going through. On the other hand, instead of trying to remember what Gregory's touch was like, why not let him touch you and experience what it feels like now? That's all I am saying, Kelsey. As your friend and your doctor, please accept my advice; you have to move forward. Think of it this way, if you were an actor who wanted to become a superstar, but you haven't landed a speaking role in fifteen years, do you continue pursuing a dream that is not supporting you, or would you set a realistic timeframe? Let's say one year, and if after that year passes, wouldn't you reevaluate if you should pursue a different vocation?"

"That's not like my situation at all! I didn't choose to be this way," I yelled at her.

"Answer my question! That would be insane to some degree, right?"

"Oh, great, now I'm insane!" I threw my arms up in the air as if I were about to fight her.

"Answer the question!" She slammed both hands down on the desk. We both just stood there breathing heavy and staring at each other. I didn't answer. I thought she calmed down, but she just thundered on.

"At some point, you have to admit to yourself that maybe being a superstar wasn't the way you were supposed to live your life. Maybe there is a higher purpose to your existence that you cannot see because you are stuck chasing after a fool's dream. I disagree. It is very similar to what you just said. You have not even considered the fact that you may never get your memory back, and you've made no preparations, no timelines, nothing to be proactive in the event that this is just your lot in life. You just keep waking up every day, and in my opinion—my professional opinion—your behavior is unrealistic."

"That is so unfair, Jamie."

"What? How is that unfair? You have been paying me, and I have been willingly doing the best job that I can to help you in this situation. Nevertheless, my diagnosis as of today is that there's nothing I can do to help you or your condition if you refuse to take a realistic approach to the situation."

"I thought your job was to listen to me so that I can get my thoughts in order, so that I can come to some kind of conclusion, whatever it may be, on my own. Not bully me into being what you want me to be."

"My job is to assist you in any way I can. How am I assisting you if I just sit here and not interject my honest and professional opinion that I believe would be best for you?"

"Maybe it's time I see another therapist," I said trying to hurt her. She looked at me with seething eyes. Her arms were still on her desk, and her tiny frame was hunched over it. She looked like a cat on its haunches ready to thwart off an enemy.

"Kelsey, any other doctor would be happy to prescribe you some Prozac and send you on your way."

Was that appropriate? Should I be on drugs, I thought?

"If you don't sit down and consider all of your options, many people are going to suffer." She had regained her composure. "If you don't do this immediately, Kelsey, you're gonna wake up one day and you'll be 60 years old. You will have missed your entire life, the opportunity to truly enjoy your life with those beautiful little boys, and your man will have left you. Is that what you want? Is that how you want to live the rest of your life?"

"Of course not! But if that's the way my life is going to turn out, so be it! I don't want to keep Gregory in a relationship just for the sake of holding onto the man. I think Gregory deserves that much. I want my emotions towards everyone I know to be genuine. If not, I won't have a life. I don't want to be fake or phony or put on a show just to keep any relationship."

Chapter Twenty-Five

More Lies

Jamie had been Gregory's therapist off and on over the last couple of years, which gave him an opportunity to release stress from time to time. He had not been in to see her for many months, and after the conversation she had earlier today with Kelsey, she wanted to get a clear sense of what was on his mind.

Gregory arrived late and profusely apologized for doing so. As of late, Gregory's stress was apparent on his face. Living under the strain of Kelsey's condition, it's no wonder he was having a hard time at work. Instead of sitting behind her desk, Jamie sat casually in a chair, and he rested on the leather sofa that was on the opposite end of her office. This was no time for beating around the bush, so Jamie came out with it.

"What's going on with you? Are you gonna leave my girl?"

"I honestly don't know," he answered calmly.

"You can't leave her—she is in no condition to function without you in her life."

"Give me one reason why I should stay, because I have a long list of reasons why I should divorce her."

"Don't be silly; she needs you."

"Kelsey? Kelsey doesn't need anybody."

"All right, because you love her," Gotcha.

"I don't know if that is true or not," Gregory could tell his answer was not what Jamie had expected him to say.

"I don't believe you. Gregory, out of all the people I know, YOU are one of them! So, don't give me the tough guy act. You love the ground that woman walks on, and you know it," Gregory was not expecting her to call him out like that either.

"To tell you the truth, I'm confused. I don't know any man alive who would want to stay in a situation like this."

"That is probably true, but this is marriage; this is *your* Kelsey."

"She hasn't been my Kelsey in ages," His eyes filled with tears. "There is nothing I wouldn't do for her, but there has to be more to life than this. I need to be loved just as much as she does. I need to be held and told that I am special, *too*. When I try to do this for Kelsey, she treats me as if I annoy her. That hurts too much when you are talking about a situation that could be forever."

"Gregory, you've been so brave, so strong, and loving to your wife. However, she needs more. Why do you think there's still a wall up between you two?" Jamie asked trying to box him into a corner so she could find out what she really wanted to know. "Has Kelsey unconsciously triggered something from the past that has made her woman's intuition surface regarding your relationship?"

"Not that I know of," he innocently replied.

Jamie thought it was time to take a different approach.

"How was your sex life a few months before the accident?" Gotcha again!

"Jamie, you and Kelsey have always been tight, and I would be a fool to think that she didn't tell you everything. I'm sure you know that Kelsey and I were having some problems before all of this happened. Yet, we both had an agreement to stick it out, and work through the rough patch," he replied truthfully.

"If that is so, why would she have Joanna pack up the boys and meet her somewhere? The night of her accident, you said she had given that order. What happened between you two?" It was the first time she has questioned him in this manner.

"Jamie, I honestly don't know what happened."

"Gregory, Kelsey has been a lot of things in her life, but never unreasonable. If she had reached that boiling point, something would have had to happen between you two. What would have made her do it?" she continued to press.

"Why is everyone obsessed with the past? Can't we just let laying dogs lie?"

"Not if they are lying!" she bold stated.

"I have always been honest with you Jamie, and I respect you too much to lie to you. Neither my wife nor I were perfect in the past, but because of my vows, I forgive Kelsey of her mistakes...." Jamie interrupted.

"Why don't you trust that Kelsey will do the same for you?" Even though he had not confessed to anything, Jamie knew he was too afraid to admit any wrongdoing to her. "Not opening up, you will just be avoiding the large elephant in the middle of the room. You can't decorate it with a planter and think that no one will see it. Some things you have to confront, and other things you need to let go of. Kelsey's tapped into something that she will not let go until she gets answers. I'm not saying that you are hiding anything, but if you need to confess, and if you really want your wife back, you are gonna have to deal with it as soon as possible."

Kelsey woke up feeling odd. Why she couldn't describe, but just as you can sense the coming of spring, Kelsey walked around anticipating something. Out of all of the rooms in her enormous house, Kelsey used her home office to surf the net, and that was about it. Nevertheless, ever since she went rummaging through her desk drawers and found the paperwork regarding her bogus father, Kelsey had spent even less time in the room. Joanna had always been a great housekeeper, and as she walked into the space it looked immaculate; dust-free, and ready for her to get back to work.

After her appointment with Dr. Jamie, Kelsey came home and quickly went about her business, combing through folders and computer files. What she was looking for, she had no idea, she just knew it was time to find it. After over two hours of searching and finding nothing, Kelsey decided to call it quits. She went into the kitchen and began fixing herself a sandwich. It wasn't until she was smearing sandwich spread and layering several kinds of lunchmeat on her wheat bread did it hit her like a bolt of lightning. As a young law student, the words of Professor Evans rang true in her spirit: *When you hit a brick wall on a case, it is always helpful to review what you already know to see if you may have overlooked it.* She could hear her favorite law professor's words repeatedly in her head until she picked up the file from the investigator regarding her father. Why hadn't she thought of it before?

Gregory sat quietly wringing his fingers the same way he did years ago in the hospital patiently waiting to hear the fate of his wife. He was nervous. He had become such a different person than what he used to be. Why should he be punished now for what he had sacrificed?

Lord, I have kept my end of the bargain, he thought. I thought you forgave me. Why must I go through this again? Why must I be put back into this prison? Why must I jeopardize all that I have been in the last three years? Please spare me the pain and the guilt of my sin.

Gregory, you shall know the truth and the truth will make you free.

Without thinking, Kelsey picked up the folder that had been given to her from the investigator and dialed the phone number on the card that was stapled to the inside of the folder. As she listened to the line ringing, she realized she had no idea what she was going to say.

"Duncan Investigations," said the woman's voice on the other end of the line.

"Hi. May I speak with Patrick Duncan please?"

"Who may I say is calling?"

"Kelsey Smith-Pritchard."

"Mrs. Smith-Pritchard, how are you? It's been a while, but it is good to hear your voice again. Hold on and let me get Patrick for you," the woman politely said before placing Kelsey on hold.

Kelsey had been on hold for less than a minute when a deep manly voice came online interrupting the hold music that was playing.

"It's my favorite client! Kelsey how are you feeling, and how is the family?" asked the gentleman on the other line.

It was true; Kelsey was Sgt. Duncan's favorite client. She had hired him on several occasions to check out a lead or follow-up on witnesses the prosecution was planning to use against her clients on several cases years ago. Smith-Pritchard and Associates had helped Sgt. Duncan to retire early from the New Jersey Police Department and begin his successful private investigations practice.

"I'm well, Patrick. Forgive me if I sound aloof, but I still have not regained my memory, so I may not remember our relationship the way you do."

"That's okay, Kelsey; the main thing is that you are still here with us, right?"

"That's right."

"So, what can I do for you? Are you back to work on another high-profile case?"

"No, actually I have not returned to work as of yet, Debbie Martin is handling my cases and running the firm until I feel comfortable enough to return."

"Well, good for you. What do you need, Kelsey?"

"I found the file you gave me regarding Jay Smith, and I was wondering; did I ever have you work on any other cases that involved any other members of my family?"

NO! I won't do it! If there is any hope of me being able to restore my marriage, I won't jeopardize it by bringing up things I can't change. I am not responsible for the actions of others, only for mine, and I have atoned. I believe that I have been forgiven, and I should only focus on forward movement. Gregory thought further.

You just said you don't know if you wanted to stay in this marriage, so if that is true, why not confess? Why not start your new life with a clean slate? Besides, true forgiveness allows the person you wronged to forgive you. If you don't want to let go of your marriage, then you must give Kelsey an opportunity to forgive you. If you think you want to let go of your marriage, then you should stop lying to yourself because you know you don't.

Sgt. Duncan had been anticipating this day for a long time. It was true he did look into another personal case for his favorite client and did not like what he had found. How he would love to expose Gregory for what he truly was. Having been faithfully married for over 25 years to his beloved Carola, Sgt. Duncan felt Gregory should get what he deserved for being so cruel to a woman that wanted nothing but to trust him. He knew how upset Kelsey was when he dropped off the package of his findings which included surveillance photos and audio. Even with the evidence in his hand, and the numerous times he had delivered proof to other spouses ever since that day, he had never seen anyone react the way Kelsey did. It truly troubled him and sent a chill up his spine.

As much as he knew Kelsey loved Gregory, she was neither upset nor out of character when presented with the information. It was no secret that Kelsey could be a hot-head, but when she viewed the photos of Gregory romantically involved with several women in three months, she remained cool as a cucumber. However, there was a glimmer in her eye that he had seen on countless occasions throughout his 20-something years on the police force. It was the cool hint of revenge, or even worse, murder. It shined so brightly in Kelsey's eyes that his uneasiness prompted his decision to follow her as she sped away from her house. She left the house and jumped into her car so quickly that he was hoping she would not do something stupid.

Unbeknownst to Kelsey, Sgt. Duncan had been driving closely behind her Mercedes. He had witnessed Kelsey argue with other drivers and swerve in and out of her lane. If it weren't for some guy in the green Toyota cutting him off, he would have been able to drive up next to her vehicle, flag her down, and get her to pull over. The next thing he knew, she swerved over into an eighteen-wheeler's path causing it to crash into her convertible. Kelsey's car was so twisted and mangled that it is only by the hand of God that saved his favorite client's life.

As Sgt. Duncan pulled his car over to see if Kelsey was still alive, he quickly punched the numbers to emergency and requested medical assistance. As he approached the scene of the accident, he could see that there were scattered photos, notes, and other debris which led a trail to Kelsey's car. She must have been driving with the folder of evidence in the other front seat. Yet, he was not expecting to see the shiny object that was glimmering at the bottom of the overturned vehicle. Sgt. Duncan never felt so guilty. Could his hunger to find out whether a husband was cheating destroy a family forever? He refused to let Kelsey's professional reputation be dishonored, so he quickly picked up all of the evidence.

Once he knew that Kelsey was safely being taken to the hospital, he said hello to a couple of old law enforcement buddies that were covering the scene accident, gave a statement, and headed back to his office. A stickler for retaining evidence records, Sgt. Duncan had done something he never thought he would ever do. He placed all of the contents of the Smith-Pritchard file in a trashcan, threw in his cigar, set it aflame, and put the gun in his top desk drawer.

Gregory what is it gonna be? Are you ready to confess your sin? "Jamie, thank you for giving me some time to consider my marriage and what it is that I want. The truth of the matter is that I will continue to fight for my Kelsey and our marriage. She is the one for me; I knew that the moment we first spoke in the bar. I knew it the day she walked down the aisle towards me; it's always been Kelsey. I just want her to love me back, to live for me the way I live for her." The admission of the truth had set him free. It was clear to Gregory that the confession of his love for Kelsey was all he needed to move forward. He had to confess that the reason he had chosen to turn his life around was not based on a condition of wanting to repair where he had gone astray, but a covenant between spirit, heart, and body, all of which belonged to Kelsey.

It didn't matter to Jamie that Gregory never admitted his secret. All that mattered was that he was willing to move forward in his marriage. Jamie was now ready to present the knowledge that she had been hiding all of these years; she never felt more ready. Jamie knew it was time because she was completely ready to divulge what she had locked away in the recesses of her mind for so long.

"Kelsey, I have done so many cases for you in the past it's hard to remember all of them. The case regarding Jay Smith is the only one that is so memorable because it led me to a dead end. That is the only personal case I can remember doing for you." Sgt. Duncan didn't think of what he just said as a lie, but rather strategic positioning. Let the past be the past.

Chapter Twenty-Six

Can You Forgive Me?

Kelsey sat in her office and let out a long sigh of relief. The last thing she needed right now was to be sleeping with the enemy. Knowing that her husband cheated on her would have been too devastating for Kelsey to bear. She didn't need that kind of betrayal even though she was expecting the worst possible report from Patrick Duncan. *Or was she hoping for the worst?* How easy it would have been to be able to justify her behavior in the past three years. She would have been able to admit that the feeling gnawing in her spirit was correct and that she wasn't crazy. However, with all of that behind her, no more drama and no more excuses. *Kelsey, it's time for you to decide what you are going to do. Are you willing to put aside your own selfish needs and hold onto the past, or do you move forward knowing that your past is of no consequence? Are you ready to allow your husband and yourself to enjoy the fullness of your marriage?* It was no getting around it. It was time to grow up and face the truth. I'm never going to get my memory back!

Kelsey mulled these thoughts over and over in her head as she took a shower. *What is it that I want? What can be salvaged after all the pain she put Gregory through? Was divorce an option?* To be truthful, Kelsey didn't know anymore. She had been living with one agenda for so long that switching direction seemed almost impossible. With how Kelsey has been behaving all of these years, it would be her fault if her husband did leave her—and he had every reason to. The biggest question Kelsey had to answer was if she was willing to try. Sticking her head out of the shower door, Kelsey could have sworn she heard the telephone ring, but maybe it was just her imagination.

On the drive home, Gregory tried to reach Kelsey, but she didn't answer the phone. He punched in a second set of numbers, but her cell phone just rang as well. He decided to check in with his mother-in- law to see if she might be there picking up the boys.

"Hey, Gregory—no, I haven't heard from Kelsey all day. But that is not surprising. She didn't mention when she would be picking up the boys, so I assumed that they would be spending the night."

"Would you mind, Mom? I want to spend some time alone with my wife tonight," Gregory confessed.

"Well, well—are you going to finally put her in her place?' Kerri-Claire giggled.

"Yes, ma'am, I am!" he exclaimed boldly.

"I pray you get your wife back, and that we can all move forward as one big happy family," she said encouragingly.

"I'll do my part, the rest will be up to you, Mom," Gregory offered not holding back.

"I know, Gregory. I know son. (*beep)*—that's my line gotta go."

Thank goodness for call waiting, Kerri-Claire thought. She was so excited to get out of their conversation that she barely heard her son-in-law say, 'Thanks, Mom.' She didn't want to get into any deep conversations, and she was tired of feeling beaten over the head. She knew she would have to talk to her daughter, and though she was not looking forward to the conversation, it had to be done. She should have done it years ago, but she was afraid of looking like a liar and the fraud that she was. She was not proud of changing her name or making up Jay Smith. The last time she talked about Junior, she was crying on the shoulder of her cousin Pauline the night she arrived in New Orleans. She had not even whispered his name again since that night. She had spent all of her life hating him. However, making up Jay Smith from a collection of stolen moments with Junior Watkins soothed her broken heart.

The one thing she never expected had been the cure. She had spent all of her life avoiding the "Junior" conversation, but she never expected it to heal her. As the painful memories were vocalized, the light in her dimly lit broken heart returned. She could literally feel the puss corroded around her contorted heart ooze out of every crevice and began pumping life into the decomposed organ. By the time she had come clean, she was free. For over thirty-eight years, she had carried a burden that had enslaved her and hadn't allowed her to pursue love again. She threw herself into her work at the convalescent home and enjoyed taking care of the elderly patients. She was safe there, never having to worry about meeting a man there who would mistreat her. She could afford a comfortable life for her and her daughter, and she had given her body into the throws of celibacy.

She was so thrilled to have two grandsons. There would be no worry of them coming home pregnant and she vowed to help raise them into responsible and respectful young men. Besides, Kerri-Claire didn't want Kelsey to go through the painful mother-daughter relationship that she had to endure with her. She never wanted to cause Kelsey any heartache, but the tinge of her own shame was too much for her to share. It kept her bound to an imaginary world, a world that let her escape with the idea of Jay Smith, and that had been enough for her all of these years.

Gregory pulled into the garage and grew more anxious when he saw Kelsey's car parked in their three-car garage. It was time to man-up, and he was actually looking forward to finally confessing his many indiscretions to his wife. Knowing the risk, he would be posing on his marriage, having the truth out in the open was the only way to try and save it. If he lost her, then it would be just punishment. If she forgave him and agreed to work through the hurt and pain of his admission, he would have an opportunity to properly make it up to her. Either way, he was no longer afraid of the consequences.

As he rehearsed his admission in his head, he was completely speechless when he walked into the house to find a candle-filled family room and Kelsey standing in the middle of the open walkway greeting him in peach-colored lingerie. The color glimmered magnificently against her bronze skin in the candlelight, and her hair was curled in big loopy curls. She looked beautiful.

"Hello, honey," Kelsey greeted him in her sweetest voice. She assumed he liked what he saw because he didn't respond. He just stood there with his eyes bulging and his mouth wide open. "Love is everything, alright?" she asked as she approached him.

Gregory was too paranoid to respond, fearing that he would ruin the mood, but he knew he was going to have to continue with the task at hand. Still, he stood there and drank in the amorous moment.

"Daddy, can you forgive me?" she spoke in a sultry tone as she stood face to face with her man. "I have been so self-centered during this entire period, not willing to consider what I know you need. I apologize," Kelsey whispered her confession in his ear, letting her breath faintly brush against his left lobe.

What was he to do? He had come home intending to make his confession known, and here was his wife trying to seduce him. Should he stop her and put at risk the one thing he had been covering up for the last three years? Kelsey was seductively speaking to him in one ear, and sweet words of wisdom were clearly audible in the other.

Your choice of wanting to tell your wife the truth and the admission of the truth to yourself has made you free.

He believed that he was given another chance to begin again, so he slid his arms around Kelsey's waist and kissed her. *Lord, thank you for putting a ram in the bush.*

Kelsey surrendered to his tender touch, closed her eyes, and let go. They made love and it was divine. For the first time ever, Kelsey was happy she had no previous memory to compare their tender moment to.

Chapter Twenty-Seven

The Car Accident

I don't know why Jamie summoned me to her office on one of our off days. I was sitting in a chair outside of her office area as my Mentor had suggested making sure that I was prepared to receive whatever Jamie had to tell me.

"She could have called me to apologize or to see how I was doing. Why do I need to make a trek all the way down to her office? I don't want to get into another fight, and I'm sick and tired of crying all of the time. I don't think I have any tears left," I admitted.

"Why do you automatically think the worse of every situation?" he asked.

"I don't know."

"Just go and talk to her. See what she wants, and instead of talking, listen to what she has to say. Go with an open mind."

"You're right. You're always right."

"I don't want to always be right. I want *you* to be right."

"Thanks." He always has a way of making me feel better.

"By the way, when you get there, take a moment to think about all of the good that has come out of three years of sessions. Sit outside of her office and just meditate about all of the discoveries you two made together in that office. Try to appreciate that, and don't beat yourself up about what you have not done, rather focus on what steps you have to take to move forward."

So, here I am trying to get a mental picture of what my life has been like over the last three years. It's hard skipping past all of the arguments and the tears that have been shed, but I am trying to focus. The only thing that seemed like progress was the fact that I had met and developed a close relationship with my Mentor. I had the support of Isabel and Moriah, and there was the faint memory of my grandfather. Not to mention, the wonderful relationship I have cultivated with my children. I could now include last night's romp with Gregory on the list. I was planning to meditate on these thoughts in case I had to do a little daydreaming in Jamie's office to make sure that I wouldn't get upset.

"I can do this. Every single encounter with someone doesn't have to be volatile." With that, I got up, tossed my hair, popped a stick of gum in my mouth, and walked into Jamie's waiting area.

"Hello, Mrs. Smith-Pritchard," her assistant greeted me. Here was my chance to respond.

"Hi, how are you, Cynthia?"

"I'm doing well—extremely well. Thanks for asking. I'll let Dr. Jamie know you are here."

I sat down, grabbed a magazine even though I had not planned to read it. I pulled out a small piece of paper from my suit jacket pocket and read it. *Tact Is The Ability To Close Your Mouth Before Someone Else Wants To.* Then there was another one. *To Handle Yourself Use Your Head, To Handle Others Use Your Heart.* I can do this. I know I can.

"Kelsey, Dr. Jamie is ready for you. You may go in."

I could only mouth the word "Thanks" because I was still reciting the text of the tiny piece of paper in my head. Here we go.

"Kelsey, it's good to see you." She walked over to me and hugged me. I responded by putting my arms around her significantly shorter frame, and I could not seem to let go. Tears were streaming down my face already. Who turned on the water?! She squeezed me back just as hard, and I could hear her sobbing, too. We just stood in the middle of her office for a moment having a little sob fest. I pulled away first. I looked her straight in the eyes, said I was sorry, truly sorry, and resumed hugging and crying some more. It felt good to release all of the pain and confusion that I had been carrying around.

She mumbled she was sorry too, and we just kept on crying for what seemed like forever. Today I know I discovered true "girl-friendship," and there was nothing like it.

"So, what have you been doing lately? How have you been?" I asked, not wanting to talk about myself on this visit. Since I was here on an off doctor-patient day, I assumed that we could just talk as friends.

"Well, I've been doing a lot of thinking and praying about our last conversation, and once again, I am sorry. I had no right to enforce my opinions on you whether they are personal or professional. I've realized that I wasn't being the best friend I had always envisioned myself to be."

This was interesting. In three years, I can't remember a time that I ever heard Jamie talk about her feelings. It felt good that this visit would be a friendly one.

"I have been doing a lot of soul searching and realized that though I know somewhere in me I was doing everything with the best of intentions, I forgot what was most important. That is that you survived a horrible car accident, and I didn't lose my sister." As she spoke she turned toward her window next to her desk and stared at her reflection. She paused for a moment, then quickly spun around towards me. Here it comes.

"Kelsey, it has come to my attention that I owe you another apology. Not for my behavior the last time we saw each other, but for taking advantage of you, and your condition." What was she talking about?

"I don't understand, Jamie. What do you mean?"

"All of my life I've leaned on you and your friendship for support. You were always there to pick up the pieces of my shattered life, and here was my chance to reciprocate. Somewhere along the way, my intentions became something else." Whoa. That was big. Didn't my Mentor tell me something like that about Jamie weeks ago? She paused. I went over to her and put my arms around her shoulders.

"It's okay."

"For once in our relationship, I felt that you truly needed me, and I finally realized all of these years I thought that I needed your friendship more than you needed mine. So here was my big chance to help you, and I feel like an idiot for mistreating our friendship and using my position as a doctor to be manipulative. It was my professional duty to maintain an objective viewpoint about your situation, and lately, it seems as if I have been only relating to you in a personal manner. That would have been fine if we were on the phone, but while you are in my office I should have had a more professional attitude. Forgive me?"

"You had me at 'I'm Sorry!'" Having just recently rented Jerry McGuire, I repeated the infamous line jokingly, trying to lighten the mood so that she wouldn't feel beaten up. She cracked up.

"You're bananas."

"So can we grab lunch or get a manicure. After that speech, I think we need to do something really girly to bond or something."

"Actually, I have something to give you."

"Presents? I like presents!" I laughed.

"Umm...I wouldn't call it a present, but I want to return something to you." She went behind her desk and pulled out a large, padded Jiffy envelope. As she handed it to me, I could see that it had my name on it and had the Clay Memorial Hospital seal as well.

"This looks official," I said in my most professional tone continuing to joke. "What's in it?" I asked, shaking it, and hearing its contents rattle around inside.

"Kelsey, that envelope contains loose items that were found either in your car or around the scene of the accident. I sealed its contents into that envelope when the police gave them to me at the hospital," I just sat there with wide eyes looking at it. Why hadn't she given it to me before? She read my mind.

"I never gave it to you or Gregory because I felt that I should hold on to it in case you got your memory back."

"What's in it?"

"Open it and see."

As I tore it open and looked inside, I could see there were about ten or so items. I began pulling them out and arranging them by size on Jamie's desk to see if I would remember anything, but nothing looked familiar. Its contents were dirty and looked as if they survived a war. They included: Two lipstick holders, one three-year-old parking ticket, loose change in the amount of $2.34

One small spray can of vanilla air freshener One removable car CD player with six CDs One cassette tape

Four pens with green and purple ink

One plastic double-sided rearview mirror frame with pictures of my kids on one side and Gregory on the other

One broken cellular earphone and car charger One business card for Duncan Investigations

"Do any of these items look familiar to you, Kelsey?"

"No, they don't. Well...the business card is for the private investigator's company I hired to look for my father. Should they? Nothing looks special. Why did you feel that you should hold them or not give them to Gregory? I mean it looks like a bunch of old stuff. Has this ticket been paid?"

"Yes. I took care of the ticket for you."

"Thanks." There was an awkward silence. I kept looking at the items hoping something would ring a bell or jog my memory, but nothing happened. "I don't get it Jamie. What is so special about all of this stuff?"

"Why don't you look at the CDs and see if they mean anything to." As I tried to get the CDs out of the CD holder I broke a nail.

"That's gonna cost you $5.00 to replace that tip crazy lady!"

"Why do I have to pay for it you broke it?" she laughed.

"What do I care about some old CDs I haven't listened to in over three years?"

"Hmmmm…I just thought you might be interested to see what kind of music you liked," she replied smugly. I grinned sheepishly.

"Okay, you got me." As I continued to pry the CDs out of the broken player it was clear I had eclectic taste. There were albums by Sarah McLaughlin, Carly Simon, Annie Lennox, Anita Baker, Seal, and a compilation album one called Maidservants. I think I saw the case for Maidservants at home.

"Nothing?"

"Nothing."

"What is the tape of?"

"Let see. Looks like House of Faith but the paper is peeled off so I can't see of what. Is this a tape from my grandfather's church?"

"I think so. I believe your mother gave it to you as a wedding present. The topic is about the roles in a marriage."

"No more cat and mouse games. Can you just tell me what you know?" As Jamie began speaking I tried hard to picture her words.

*"On the day of your accident, you called me at my office giving me the scoop on a deal you just clos*ed."

"Congrats! I'm so proud of you! We should all go out to celebrate. Have you told Gregory yet?"

"Not yet, I can't reach him."

"Tell me about the meeting."

You began to tell me how you were sitting with a bunch of stiff shirts around a big table working on a merger deal for a client. I never could understand how you could work with such uptight stuffy people who thought that the sun and moon revolved around them and made a point to tell you so constantly.

"Because I like sending them to you for therapy after I've taken every last penny from them."

"You're sick, you know that, right?"

"I know. You should have seen me. Right in the middle of closing this deal, this creep from the other side, Victor Onidal, tried to belittle me right in the middle of the meeting, questioning why their team should do business with my firm since we hadn't completed many acquisitions deals before. He rambled on about not knowing anything about me, and so on, and so on."

"How did you deal with that?"

"I politely told him that I was sorry his team had not done their due diligence as they could have Googled me at any time!"

"You are too much!" she gasped. "What did he say or do after that?"

"I didn't give him a chance to say anything. I closed by saying, 'Look gentlemen, don't waste my time! I am cute, and I am not used to hearing the word 'no,' so do we have a deal or what?' The room busted out with laughter."

"No, you didn't!"

"Yes, I did, and with a straight face to boot! It lightened the mood, we all laughed, creepy Victor apologized, and we moved on to close the deal.

"Unbelievable. Where are you headed now?"

"I'm going to hit the spa, but first I'm running home to leave a note for Gregory and have Joanna make the kids dinner. Want to join me at the spa? My treat!"

"I should be treating you, but I've got clients today." "Stack 'em and rack 'em, huh?"

"That's me. There are a lot of needy people out there and 'who are they gonna call?'" she sang to the melody of Ghostbusters.

"Jamie Hyman! I'll call you back later."

"Tata big shot."

"*I was just finishing up with my patient, Mr. Newman, when I got a frantic call from you. My assistant Cynthia came into my office and interrupted my session, which is unacceptable, so I knew this must have been an emergency.*"

"What's wrong, Kelsey? Calm down I can't hear you. Kelsey, calm down and try to speak clearly. Kelsey, are you there?

"I am so sick and tired of his BS. I can't take this anymore, Jamie! I won't let my kids be subjected to his unscrupulous behavior, and I refuse to let anybody do this to me!"

"What are you talking about? What did Gregory do?"

"I am not gonna sit here and be married to this man anymore. I'm tired of playing games and living a charade. I don't deserve this! No more! And to make matters worse…use your blinker idiot! I'm not a mind reader you know!"

"Where are you right now, Kelsey?"

"I'm on the Turnpike."

"Why? Where are you going?"

"I just had to get out of the house. I am going to check into a hotel, and that's it. I'm not going back home! Drive! Please try driving!"

"Kelsey, I was so confused. I had no idea what was going on, and you kept screaming at people to drive faster. You were crying frantically, and it sounded as if you were drunk. We had just spoken about an hour and a half before, so I knew that wasn't the case, but you were hysterical. In the background, I could hear your House of Faith tape playing. The preacher was delivering a powerful message."

"Wives submit to your own husbands…" the preacher said.

"In between sobs, you would scream frantically at the tape as if you were talking to him directly."

"For the husband is the head of the wife…."

"You mean to tell me that I'm supposed to submit myself to a man I am more educated than and out-earn? A man who walks around like Mr. Magoo, and takes advantage of every single last thing that I've done for this family? A man who holds onto his childish ways instead of growing up and being the head of his household? You're telling me that I'm supposed to honor this man no matter what he does, even if he doesn't benefit this family? I'm supposed to submit myself to a man who takes advantage of my feelings, disregards anything that is going on in my life, and disrespects me every chance he gets? I'm supposed to honor a man who wants to work all of the time and spend no time with his children? I should honor this, especially after what I found out today?"

"Kelsey, what did you find out today?"

"You want to know what happened or what is happening right now? Well, I'll tell you; I am leaving Gregory, and I've had enough of his crap! I'm taking my babies, and we are going to stay in a hotel until I can get settled. I don't need this mess, the drama, and I don't have to put up with his selfish ways. I refuse to be disrespected!"

"Girlfriend, what happened?"

"No matter how many times I asked, you would not fill in the blanks as to what had happened. Then you got so quiet I couldn't tell if you were there or if I had lost you. Then I heard the preacher's thunderous voice in the background still delivering his message."

"Men, love your wives, just as Christ also loved the church and gave Himself for her."

"Is that all you got? Why aren't men ordered to submit to us, and the family? I don't need his love if he can't submit to the concept of being a husband and all that it requires…get out of my way! Drive you moron!"

"Kelsey, where are you?"

"I'm on the freeway driving towards the airport with a bunch of Sunday-drivers!"

"Where are the kids?"

"I've arranged for Joanna to pick them up and bring them to me. I don't want them to see me like this. They shouldn't see their mother as a crying mess!"

"Kelsey, I want you to do something, so listen very carefully. Take your time, slow down, and pull over to the right-side meridian so you can calm down and tell me what is going on. Did you hear me, Kelsey?"

"I had never heard you like this before. You were despondent and driving like a crazy woman."

"Kelsey? Did you hear what I just said?"

"Between your sobs, you answered yes, and said you were pulling over."

"Get out of my way you idiot! I am so tired of stupid men. Same to you!"

"What is going on?"

"Some guy is calling me names!"

"I am not crazy; you just can't drive!"

"Slow down and let him pass so you can get over!"

"He's in the lane to my left. Yeah, well back at you stupid!"

"Kelsey, focus on getting over."

"Witnesses said that you just swerved over without looking. I heard a Mac truck's horn, screeching brakes, and the preacher in the background."

"So, husbands are to love their own wives as their own bodies; he who loves his wife loves himself."

"KELSEY!"

"JAMIE!"

"The last thing I heard was you calling my name. To my horror, the next thing I heard was the metal of your car being crushed by an eighteen-wheeler."

She began crying as if it had just happened.

"I heard glass flying and you screaming, then my assistant started praying loudly, and I was paralyzed. The last thing I heard was the preacher saying," she finished,

"A man who finds a wife finds a good thing and obtains favor from the Lord."

Chapter Twenty-Eight

It All Makes Sense!

I just sat there with my mouth hanging open. So many things were running through my mind. So many questions I wanted to ask, but Jamie was a mess. She was sitting across from me at her desk shaking and crying. Her head was in her hands, and she was crying so hard that her entire face had turned red. I got up to comfort her, and she looked up at me and started crying harder. Had she really carried the pain of this experience around for three years? What would I have done if the situation were reversed? I couldn't even imagine being on the other line as my best friend's vehicle was being crushed by a large truck. My heart began beating faster just at the thought of it. I reached over to grab some tissue for Jamie, and she just collapsed into a heap of quivering flesh.

As her assistant walked in, I was so thankful that I had been nice to her today. All of these years I had treated her as if she were insignificant, when in fact, her prayers may have been the reason I was still here. It's funny how things turn out.

"She's been holding in those tears for so long," Cynthia confirmed. It might not have been the best time to discuss this, but I had to know. "Cynthia, you were there, right?" I asked already knowing the answer.

"Yes, I was."

"Would you mind telling me what happened after the crash?"

"If Dr. Jamie doesn't mind?" Jamie nodded.

Cynthia began, "*As you can imagine, we were both startled and scared for you. I immediately started praying...*"

"Thank you," I interrupted.

"No need to thank me. That's just who I am," she replied kindly, and I believed her. It explains why she has such a calm and amazingly peaceful demeanor about her.

"KELSEY! KELSEY, CAN YOU HEAR ME?" Jamie let out a blood-curdling yell. Her poised and cool professional demeanor was gone. Though heavily in prayer, Cynthia had made that mental note. She knows how close Jamie was to Kelsey, even though she could never figure out why.

"KELSEY, CAN YOU HEAR ME? ARE YOU ALL RIGHT?" The phone went dead. "OH, MY GOODNESS!"

As she dialed 911, Jamie had never been overly religious, but she could appreciate Cynthia covering her best friend in prayer. She had been to church a couple of times with Kelsey and Mom over the years, but she never really leaned on any sort of faith. But if anyone needed prayer right now, it was Kelsey.

"Yes, I'd like to report an accident on New Jersey Turnpike South. The accident would be with a gold-colored Mercedes, and I think a truck. There may have been other cars as well. How do I know all of this? I was just on the phone with my sister while she was in the car, and I could hear the accident from her phone. Hurry, please, it sounded horrible! She was on her way downtown, so I would assume she should be between Exits 16 and 14. Oh, someone just called it in, and you know where she is located? They are already on the scene of the accident? Thank God! Which hospital will the paramedics be taking her to? Clay Memorial? I'm on my way. Thanks for all of your help."

"Kelsey, that's all I know from the phone conversation. After that, Jamie flew out of the office. I can only assume that she called your mom and husband."

When Cynthia finished, Jamie tried to compose herself so that she could finish telling the ordeal. Cynthia got up to get Jamie something to drink, and Jamie requested some Tylenol as well. After Jamie consumed both, she took a moment to clean herself up. I just sat with her and waited patiently for her to speak. I smoothed her hair off of her face, and she began to speak without looking at me.

"I'm sorry that I just fell apart on you, but I had not dealt with those emotions from that day until now."

"Don't be sorry. I don't know how anyone could have held on to that without telling anybody."

"I didn't have time, Kelsey. A million things were running through my mind. Of course, my first thought was wondering whether you were okay. Then I had to try to contact Mom and Gregory, all the while wondering what the heck had happened between the two of you. As I drove over to the hospital, I decided not to badger him for answers, though I wanted to wring his neck for hurting you. Mom, of course, was a wreck, and I had to calm her down long enough so that she could get in the car and drive safely over to the hospital. I asked her to stay at home until I had more news, but she, of course, was not going for that. I could not catch Gregory on his cell, but I finally reached him at home.

"Hello."

"Gregory, its Jamie. Where are you?" I asked fishing to see what kind of temperament he was in. Since you never told me what happened between you two, I didn't know if you guys had words or not.

"I'm at the house. Have you talked to Kelsey?"

"Why, Gregory?"

"I need to ask her why my nanny was instructed to pack an overnight bag and take my kids to some hotel. Do you know what's going on with her? I haven't talked to her all day, but I can see that she called my cellular several times. Then, I come home, and this is going on."

"Gregory…"

"Hold on, Jamie. Joanna, I haven't talked to my wife, and I don't know what is going on." Gregory stated while trying to stop his nanny from packing the kids' overnight bag.

"But, Mr. Pritchard, your wife told me to do so," Joanna calmly replied, still folding clothes and placing them into the bag.

"I don't care what my wife instructed you to do. You are not permitted to take my kids anywhere. Matter of fact, you're fired! Get your stuff and get out of my house!" Gregory shouted, throwing the overnight bag at the wall.

"Gregory, wait a minute! Kelsey has been in a car accident, and they are taking her to Clay Memorial," Jamie announced.

"Kelsey's been in an accident? How bad was it? Is she okay, Jamie? Which hospital? Hold on, Joanna. Kelsey's been in a car accident. I need you to stay here with the kids while I go and make sure she is okay. Don't leave the house. I will call you to let you know what's going on. Let the kids play in the backyard, and don't say anything until I call you. Got it?"

"Yes, Mr. Pritchard. Does this mean I'm not fired?" "Yes, Joanna, it does."

"Did Gregory ever mention why I was mad at him?"

"Kelsey, if I were to ask him right now, he has no clue as to what was going through your head. And I believe him. Since you can't remember anything, no one knows what was going on that day."

"Well, let's just call Mr. Pritchard and tell him everything you know to make him confess what he did, and just get it out in the open!" That sounded logical to me. What was he hiding all of these years?

"Kelsey, with all you know about Gregory right now, does it matter?"

"Of course, it does! Maybe I don't know as much as I think I know about him." Again, that was logical.

"Kelsey, are you sure you want to go down that road?"

"What do you mean? Anything that can help me get over these last couple of years of confusion would be helpful, don't you think? If there is something I need to know about Gregory, something that will let me know his true character, I want to know!" I was getting heated, and I reached for the phone on Jamie's desk and started dialing his cell. Jamie grabbed the phone and hung it up.

"Kelsey, I just heard how well you and Gregory have been doing. How you're both trying to take it slow but have committed to moving forward with the relationship as husband and wife. Why do you want to go backward?"

Wait a minute. I didn't tell her what happened last night or, that I had newfound feelings for my husband.

"Where did you get your information from?" I asked, trying to stay calm.

"Gregory, of course."

"What? When did you have time to talk to Gregory?"

"He was so happy about last night that he called me this morning and told me the good news."

"It's barely noon! What did he do, roll off of me and dial your number?"

"Kelsey, I have been seeing Gregory as a patient since your accident. Did you think he was not in therapy?"

"I knew that he had seen a shrink a couple of times, but I never knew it was you!"

"You sound as if that is a problem?"

"IT IS! How can you remain neutral? You just admitted earlier that you had let the personal and professional get in the way of how you counseled me! Here you are playing both sides of the fence. All this time, I thought you were trying to help me, but how do I know you weren't trying to just help Gregory and his motives?"

"I HAVE stayed neutral when dealing with both of you. I have given both of you the best individual advice—working for one common good. We are a family, and I tried to do my best to hold the two of you together all of these years—trying to get both of you to work past your individual issues for the sake of the marriage, and your kids. Don't you understand that?"

"Are you speaking as my doctor or his?"

"I am speaking as your sister!" I could see Cynthia slinking out of the room out of the corner of my eye.

"So, you mean to tell me, in all of your sessions, Gregory never admitted to doing anything that was wrong?"

"Nothing that would explain why you would want to leave him."

"Then he is just a bold face liar! Was I so unrealistic and unreasonable that I would want to pick up everything and leave my husband?" Kelsey asked perplexed.

"That's what's so puzzling. You weren't perfect, but you were never unrealistic. You have always been very methodical and reasonable," she responded.

"Was I having an affair?" I asked just in case I had to face the fact that the problem was me.

"You? No, never! That's not who you were."

"Then there's only one way to find out what the heck was going on! Let's get him on the phone right now!" She startled me when she pulled the phone away from me and threw it on the floor.

"WHAT'S YOUR PROBLEM?!"

"My problem is that you never answered my questions. Now let's just calm down, and let's talk."

"Only after you answer one question for me."

"Fair enough. What is it?"

"Did you ever sleep with Gregory?"

"What? Girlfriend, you better start smoking the good crack!"

"Is that a yes or a no?"

"IT'S A NEVER, EVER WOULD I. OR COULD I, DO SOMETHING LIKE THAT WITH ANY MARRIED MAN, AND ESPECIALLY NOT YOURS!" She was breathing hard trying to catch her breath after she yelled out her answer. I calmed down.

"Well, I just had to ask!" I snapped back in a lower tone.

"Look, Kelsey, I've known you both for so long, do you think I want you guys to divorce? When I stood as your Maid of Honor, I took my vows, too. I vowed as a participating witness that I would make sure that you guys stay together. It is my job, and everyone who attended your wedding, to assist in any way possible to make sure you hold on to your vows, and I will. Now, if I can do that by counseling both of you, as any other marriage counselor would, then I will. Don't get mad at me for trying."

"I apologize, but it caught me off guard. I was angry that you knew we had consummated our marriage before I had a chance to tell you."

"Get over it, Kelsey. Gregory's been confiding in me for years. He told me he was falling in love with you long before he confessed it to you. He even practiced proposing to you with me as your stand-in before he asked your mother. Not to mention, I went with him to pick out your ring. Do you think Gregory would have selected such a high-quality diamond grade without the help of a woman?"

"How should I know? I can't remember anything!" We busted up in laughter. That was a pretty stupid question. Jamie was still sniggling when she replied.

"The point is, Kelsey, I have always had your back when it came to Gregory, and he has always come to me to try to understand you better. Truth be told, it was my talking with him that made me realize that I had been so selfish. If it makes you feel any better, I will stop talking to him and counseling him and let the two of you work things out together. Or he can find another therapist if he needs to vent."

"That would be most appreciated," I replied. "It's not that I don't trust you, but I think Gregory and I need to rely on each other for a change in order to make this marriage work."

"Understood. Now back to the matter at hand, do you still think you need to know what happened over three years ago?"

I couldn't answer that question. My nose was itching to find out what the heck was going on back then. When I didn't answer right away, she spoke up.

"Kelsey, whatever Gregory was or did three years ago, he has changed. I mean out and out changed."

"Like how?"

"Well, he matured. With you out of commission, Kelsey, he had to be the head of the household."

"Was he not before?" I probed.

"It's different. You've always had a strong personality. Things have always gone your way since I've known you, and if people didn't adhere to your vision, they were steamrolled over."

"You make me sound as if I were evil."

"You weren't evil, Kelsey; you've just always had strong leadership skills and quick wit. So, when you weren't there to pick up the pieces, Gregory had to step things up for him and the children. Your accident made him responsible. The boys were pretty young, and with their mom out of commission, they needed extra attention. Your mom helped and so did I, but it was Gregory who stepped up to the plate."

"Was Gregory hen-pecked?"

"No, he wasn't. Trust me, Gregory had a quiet strength about him, and you knew very quickly if you were crossing that line. He always adored you, so he would let you get away with murder. Your dominant personality afforded you the ability to easily manipulate scenarios to work in your favor.

"So, you're saying I was evil?"

"This is not coming out right. Let me try again…"

"Oh, so you mean you want a second try at "Stump the Therapist?"

"That's what I mean!"

"Huh?"

"You were always cunning, and people liked your quick wit. That doesn't make you a bad person."

"Uh-huh."

"I believe that Gregory came to realize that he almost lost you and that life, your life together, could have been made short. While you were in your coma, Mom was freaking out, but Gregory spent the whole time on his knees praying that you would wake up. He wouldn't leave your side for a minute, and he was great with the kids," she continued. "Even when you came home from the hospital, he was such a doting and loving husband to you, and it was no act. He meant it."

"Come to think of it, I do remember overhearing Gregory praying one night while I was in the hospital."

"See what I mean."

"That was probably just his guilt kicking in," I teased. It felt good to hear Jamie speak so highly of Gregory.

"Precisely. I don't know what he did or didn't do but what I saw in Gregory were remorse and repentance. There was a newness about him that deserves to be commended. I'll pose the question a different way one more time. What matters more? Would you rather risk digging up old bones and pain in order to know what happened the day of the accident or knowing that Gregory has become the mature, loving man and attentive father that he is today because of it?"

Good question.

Chapter Twenty-Nine

Breakdown to Breakthrough

Kelsey sat in her hot car with the windows up in the hospital parking lot. She needed a moment to get a handle on what she had just learned. She felt as if last night was a big hoax. All that she had been feeling was, in fact, true. Gregory must have cheated on her. Except Patrick Duncan said he hadn't found anything. Maybe he lied or maybe nothing turned up, but something just didn't make sense. Who was the *real* Gregory, and how could he have hidden this hideous thing from her and others for so long?

Kelsey was about to spiral out of control when her cell phone rang. It was her mother.

"Hello, Mom," she managed to squeak out without sounding too upset. She was in no mood to go into this with her mother.

"Kelsey, are you busy? I really need to talk with you. Can you come over?" It took Kerri-Claire all morning to get the courage to make this call.

"Is everything okay?" Kelsey asked, half paying attention.

"Yes, I just need to get some things off my chest."

"Mom, I'm not in the mood to get into an argument with you. I have to sort out some things with Gre…"

Interrupting her daughter, Kerri-Claire refused to let her moment of bravery pass. "I don't need you to do anything but listen. I promise I'll do all the talking. I want to talk to you about your father, Kelsey."

I was shocked. "Mom, I'm on my way."

Was this too good to be true? Was my mother finally going to tell me the truth about my father or was this another lie to throw me off track? By accepting the invitation, am I opening up another wound that would lead me on another wild goose chase?

Kelsey would deal with the Gregory issue later. As a matter of fact, Gregory would be leaving this afternoon for a short business trip, so she would have to wait to confront him. On the way over to her mother's house, Jamie called.

"Kelsey, I just wanted to make sure that you are okay. Where are you? Would you like to grab something to eat so we can discuss this situation as girlfriends and not as doctor and patient?"

"I'm on Route 22 stuck in traffic. My mom called, and she wants to tell me something about my dad."

"If I can offer some advice, Kelsey, please listen to her with your heart, not with your head."

"I will."

As Kelsey pulled in front of her mother's home, it did occur to her that maybe Jamie had already spoken to her mom and knew what her mother was going to say. Well, that didn't matter now. What would usually have caused Kelsey to fume was of no consequence. All that matters is that she would hear it for herself. She was just about to get out of the car when her cell rang again.

"Hello?"

"How did everything go with Jamie today?" her Mentor asked.

"It went well. I did everything you suggested and we both apologized. Jamie told me she was on the phone with me at the time of my accident. The visit was a very emotional encounter."

"I see you don't call her Dr. Jamie anymore."

"I can't, she's my sister, and I love her very much. Hearing what she had to endure was phenomenal. I don't know if I could have handled hearing such a horrible ordeal as it was happening to my friend, and still have my wits about me. Jamie talks as if I were the strong one, but I believe she is actually the stronger one; even more so than maybe she ever realized."

"Sometimes people give others more credit than they give themselves."

"I suppose that is true. My mom called and wanted to tell me something about my father. I just pray it's not another bogus treasure hunt."

"Well, you know the first rule of a treasure hunt, don't you?"

"No."

"Never get stuck on the clues, or you'll never find the treasure."

I could see my mom sitting in her backyard as I walked into her family room. She was there waiting with a pitcher of lemonade and cookies. It was a very serene moment to see how peaceful she seemed. I knew she must have heard me walk in the house since the top corner of the front door has a little bell taped to it. It's my mom's home remedy for a security system. I walked to the back porch and sat quietly in the seat alongside her. So many things were swirling in my head, and here I was about to get a double dose of Kerri-Claire. Before walking in the door, I literally had to take a couple of deep breaths and meditate on one of my sayings I prepared for my visit with Jamie. *To Handle Yourself Use Your Head, To Handle Others Use Your Heart.*

We sat there for a while before she started to speak, and she told me what I believed to be the truth. She told me all about Junior Watkins and how he had dumped us before I was born. She told me of the disgrace that my grandfather felt after hearing the news that his daughter was pregnant. She suspected that was why my grandfather loved me so much—maybe he believed he had a second chance with Kelsey. Had he been given another chance with another little girl? She talked about how our inseparable relationship may have masked his fear of losing another baby girl to lustful temptations. She believed he spent every moment he could with me, feeling guilty for working so much when she was a little girl. It was hard for me to believe that the patriarch of the Rollins' clan would allow the guilty pleasure of the young lovers to be his motive of creating a tight knit relationship with his only granddaughter. I was told how I would fly to New Orleans to spend the summer with my family until I was in my early teens.

She explained to me that when I was in the 9th grade, telling me that her father had died was the hardest thing she ever had to do. She had assumed that I would break down sobbing hysterically at the news, but instead, I pointed to her mother laughing wildly in disbelief. So, there she was, mourning the loss of her beloved father, and now she would have to deal with the fact that her child had completely lost her mind, too. That was until she realized the date was April 1st. She explained that I had assumed she was playing an April Fool's Day joke on me. She also informed me I had never cried or mourned the death of my grandfather until a decade later. She explained that before my grandfather's funeral, I was never interested in my father or his whereabouts.

She confessed how she came up with the name Jay Smith. Her cousin Pauline called him "sh**head," among other things. On three occasions they discussed Junior after her arrival. She simply used the "J" for Junior, and the "S" from one of Pauline's colorful colloquialisms in order to make sure she wouldn't forget her make-believe husband's name. She had her name officially changed to substantiate the lie of having been married. Mom looked as if she was being freed from the pain of yesteryear. I watched her expressions carefully as she spoke without once looking at me. She sat staring at her beautiful garden, lost in a trance-like state, as I listened attentively.

After replaying the words in my head, I couldn't believe that she held onto this information for so long. I was flabbergasted that she would choose to keep her pain bottled up inside her all of these years—it's a wonder that all kinds of illnesses didn't latch onto her full-figured body. I was unable to comprehend what life must have been like to live life never wanting to feel the caress of a man ever again based on Junior's betrayal for almost 40 years. What a waste of a perfectly good woman; what a waste of a life that hasn't been able to experience the true love of a man. My heart bled for her as I reminded myself that I was headed down that same road for almost 4 years.

After she finished speaking, I reached into my purse and pulled out my brush. I grabbed one of Mom's patio barstools and pulled it behind her chair. Without thinking, I tilted her head and began to brush her long dark brown and gray strands. I could see her shoulders shrugging from crying so hard, but I continued to sweep the brush through her mane without speaking. When she was able to gain her composure, she spoke.

"I used to brush your hair whenever something bothered you. Do you remember that?"

"No, I don't."

"I'm sorry I didn't tell you sooner, Kelsey. I just didn't have the strength."

"Mom, I apologize for haranguing you about my father. I didn't know."

"It's okay. I just want to move forward and finally be free from the ghost of Junior Watkins forever."

"Mom?"

"Yes," she responded with her eyes closed, enjoying the brush's nurturing bristles.

"I want you to know that I love you for wanting to protect me from Junior; he was not worthy of our love. I also love you for having the courage to make me come here today and listen. I want you to know that I place no blame on you or the decision you made to keep the information from me because I understand that it was from a place of love. I also want you to know that your sacrifice was unbelievable. I am hoping by your being able to confide in me that we can let down our guard and have a healthy relationship. Is that possible?"

Her mom's tears answered her question.

The rest of the day was spent talking and laughing, something Kelsey didn't remember them ever doing before. Kelsey prepared steaks for them both on the grill, and they sat outside until the sun went down.

As Kelsey was about to leave, her mom said, "You give those babies a big kiss from their grandma, okay?"

"I will, and let's set up a monthly spa day just you, Jamie, and me, my treat. Deal?"

"You'll never have to twist my arm to go to the spa."

"Great. I'll make the arrangements and will keep you posted. See you soon."

When Kelsey got home, she was able to spend some time with the boys before they went to bed. She even had a moment to unwind from what started out as an emotionally charged morning to a tranquil day. However, there was still the Gregory issue. She had made amends with both her mom and Jamie, and she would have come to a definitive decision regarding how she would handle Gregory and how she would proceed before his arrival tomorrow evening.

Kelsey had meant every word she said to her mother. She did respect her mom's resolution to block out the agonizing memories of her father but was terrified that she could end up with the same kind of hate for Gregory that Mom had for Junior. It seemed almost inevitable that she, too, would choose to deny herself an opportunity to love again if she found out that Gregory did cheat on her after all. She was confused more than ever and needed sound advice. Everyone Kelsey called wasn't at home, and she didn't want to call her mom figuring that she had spent too much time on an emotional rollercoaster today. Enough running from the problem, Kelsey thought as she dialed Gregory's cell phone. He didn't answer his cell phone or the phone in his hotel room. *Great, I bet he's out on the prowl.*

That night, when her friends in the woods visited her, she quickly unloaded her suspicions about Gregory. Though she didn't have any proof, she could read the writing on the wall. They listened politely, and unlike last time, didn't have much to say.

"I can't tell you how confused I am about this whole thing," I confessed.

"So, what is your next step? Are you willing to be committed to moving forward in your marriage and stop chasing after the past?" Moriah questioned.

"I don't know. Whatever I decide, I will have to be committed to standing my ground no matter what," I proclaimed.

"That's the best you can do."

"The not knowing is the fun part, remember?" Isabel added with a smile.

"I know, I know."

Moriah began to sniggle, and it was so infectious that the two of us couldn't resist joining in. After a moment or two, the laughter subsided, and we were able to walk through this wooded paradise arm in arm enjoying the sunshine. As we enjoyed our stroll, in the distance I could see the image of the once dead dog that had gnawed on my arm hiding behind a tree up ahead.

"There's that stupid dog again!" I proclaimed.

"Where? I don't see anything," exclaimed Moriah.

"Right there, to the left, behind that skinny tree! You don't see the dog looking directly at us?"

"Kelsey, there is nothing there. The dog doesn't exist anymore," Isabel added.

"But I'm looking right at it, and it's peering at me!"

"Kelsey, it's time for us to walk you out of here? are you coming with us?" Moriah announced.

As I turned to answer her, I noticed that we were walking on a pathway that would lead me out of the woods. Why hadn't I seen it before?

"Is that how the dog got into the woods in the first place?" I was so preoccupied with the pooch that I didn't focus on the fact that I had an opportunity to be released from what had ensnared me for over three years.

"Kelsey, we can walk right out of here, but you have to make an effort to never think about the dead dog again. It is your choice."

"But it's not dead any longer. We can take it with us. It must be starving," I don't know why I kept pressing the issue.

"Either you let your past go, or we have to leave you here," Moriah sweetly sang.

"What?"

"That dog represents everything you have been holding onto, the identity of your father, your relationship with your mother, and husband. If you keep looking back, you will never be able to move forward. It's your decision, and there is a long road ahead of you. This is what you said you wanted, right? Are you coming with us or not?" Isabel was starting to get testy again.

"I'm coming."

"But can you let go of your past once you walk out of here and once you wake up?" I remembered Moriah's inquiry as I opened my eyes.

For the first time, it was clear. I sat up in my bed looking around the room trying to get my bearings, understanding that Isabel and Moriah were really extensions of my mind's eye as Jamie had once suggested. I had been having conversations in a different realm that had consoled, corrected, and nurtured me. My imagination had run wild. Were all of the symbols in my dreams trying to show me that I am truly crazy? No wonder Jamie had looked at me as if I should have been committed. Everyone else just let me ramble on about the two women. I made up friends denying a friendship that would sacrifice everything for me. What I assumed was the root of Jamie's jealousy was really her way of crying out that she too needed more of me. I felt ashamed.

It was time for me to face the truth that I must walk out of those woods forever and forget about that dumb dog or it would come back to bite me. I had to do it for my own sanity. Even though I realized that it was late in the wee hours, I had to speak with my Mentor and reached for the phone. As I did, I accidentally knocked over a book that was on my nightstand. The book fell open onto the floor with its soft cover forming a teepee beside my bed. I fumbled in the dark to reach for it but stopped when he answered the phone. I quickly explained my dream to him, and he listened quietly.

"That's it in a nutshell. Do you think I'm crazy, too?" I asked my Mentor.

"Crazy? No. Misinformed, misguided, and completely off base, yes." That was harsh.

"Okay, why that response? You have my full attention."

"While it is true that you have been wandering in the woods for almost four years, and it is time for you to move on, it was never a question of you being crazy. It was a question of whether you were ready and mature enough to accept complete deliverance from your past demons and experience the liberty of moving to a different level without having any regrets."

"Hmmm…I don't understand what you are getting at."

"This entire journey was predicated on your wanting to be able to remember and move forward at the same time, right? Well, that's an oxymoron. Too much onus had been placed on remembering and not moving forward. That's like a sick person begging to be healed but then wants to take their illness with them. It doesn't work. You had to come to a point of realizing what was more important. There is nothing wrong with learning from your history, but *your* story must continue long after the distant images of your past fades. Understand?"

"Well, sort of."

"Who you are is determined by what you are capable of doing, not what you have done, especially if there has been a significant change in the person. So many people are caught up with carrying a cross of their sins around for the rest of their lives. This type of thinking chokes the possibility of completely understanding one's true purpose and the possibility of redemption. No one said that Gregory has to walk around with an "A" on his chest for what you think he might have done, particularly if he has rectified his ways by having his actions substantiate any promises of change. Kelsey, who are you to constantly condemn him? Who allowed you to open up Gregory's closet and expose his skeletons? Just because you can't remember them doesn't mean you didn't have a few bones in the closet yourself." he finished.

"I understand," I meekly replied trying to get him to stop flogging me.

"I don't think you do," he persisted. "Kelsey, even in a court of law, you can't be tried twice for the same crime!"

I was broken, tired, and couldn't hold it any longer. The tears were flowing freely from my eyes.

"No matter what I decide, I need this pain to stop immediately. I couldn't take you or another person being mad at me. There is too much to filter through," I whined.

"Stop it, Kelsey! Get up right now and onto your feet! Stop acting like a spoiled little girl. You want to be delivered from the pain, then get up and say so! You are stronger than this. You have survived every challenge that has been thrown your way since you were a little girl, so I'm telling you I will not permit you to fail now!"

"Lord God, I'm just not strong enough, smart enough, or capable of doing it. I'm tired of going around and around this mountain again. Why can't I find out the truth about Gregory? It doesn't seem fair that he gets to walk around like Mr. Magoo but for the rest of my life, and if I choose to stay with him, I'll have this hanging over my head. Why do I have to live knowing that there is a possibility that somewhere another woman, or many women, had experienced the pleasure that I shared with *my* husband last night?" I yelled back at him and was completely shocked.

It was the first time since I heard him talk to me at my grandfather's church that I actually referred to him as anything other than my Mentor.

"My child, have you ever heard that 'to error is human but to forgive is divine.'"

"I never liked that saying," I pouted.

"Well then how about, '…forgive us our trespasses as we forgive those who trespass against us?' What good would it be for you to know every little detail of the indiscretion if you aren't incapable of forgiving Gregory for it?"

"Don't you understand? I need closure! I need peace of mind!"

"Your kind of peace of mind will have you stuck in the woods and feeding a dead dog."

"You're all knowing! Why can't you remove this burden? Tell me what happened? Why didn't you just tell me from the start?" I challenged Him. He was God and could rectify the last three years of my life with one glimpse.

"Do you think it is wise to tempt me, Kelsey?" he answered calm but sternly.

"I DON'T CARE! JUST TELL ME WHY? WHY THE ACCIDENT? WHY DID I HAVE TO LOSE MY MEMORY? WHY NOT TELL ME ABOUT GREGORY? WHY, LORD WHY?" I yelled at the top of my lungs and threw myself on the floor.

"Kelsey, I had to turn what could have been bad for good. I had to use your accident to bring a change of heart in Gregory, to finally release your mother from years of pain, and to teach Jamie not to idolize your friendship or her position. Not to mention, I had to stop you from making the biggest mistake of your life that would have ruined the lives of your sons. I had to intervene. Each of your family members were headed down a dark path to destruction that was set to destroy you. I had to use the calamity you chose to create by driving like a madwoman to conform all of you. What good am I to a praying family if I don't send liberation? So, you see, while your loved ones were focusing on you, I was working on them.

Not to mention, when Patrick Duncan gave you the truth about Gregory, you couldn't handle it. You immediately set out on a path that would have rapidly destroyed not only yourself but others as well. I had to use your anger to divert you from choosing to use the handgun you put in your purse so that you wouldn't use it on Gregory. Do you not know that the truck driver in the accident lost his life, and another family was torn apart because you carelessly veered into his lane? Did you know that Patrick Duncan took the evidence of Gregory's infidelity and the shiny gun you had with you from the crime scene to spare you any embarrassment or legal charges? Patrick destroyed all of the evidence giving Gregory a second chance even though it went against how he truly felt. Patrick was more concerned with saving your reputation than Gregory's hide!" He went on.

"So, you see Kelsey, this wasn't done to you but for you enabling you to have restored relationships with your loved ones. It was done to free your family from mistakes, wrongdoings, and years of pain. It was done to save you from doing wrong. Are you able to comprehend that by correcting Gregory, the generational curse of infidelity that has plagued his family has been eliminated from your sons, and they will now have a chance to be faithful to their wives? Now I have done as much as I can do. If you are willing and obedient, then you shall enjoy all that has been done for you and your family. Are you willing, Kelsey? Can you trust me enough to forgive Gregory without knowing the details? Are you capable of being obedient enough to follow the angels out of the woods forever?"

By the time he finished with me, I was left lying flat on my face worshipping. How much did he love me and my family that he used what should have been catastrophic for our good? With this type of spiritual spanking, the only thing I could say was…

"Toby…Lord, my name is Toby!"

After making my confession, I raised my head off of the floor, and even in the dark, I could clearly see the words on the cover of the book that had fallen, which were, *Holy Bible.*

Chapter Thirty

When I woke up the next morning, I was greeted by Gregory lying on top of me with his arms wrapped around my body.

"Good morning, baby. Did you sleep well?" he inquired sweetly as he kissed my face.

"Yes, as a matter of fact, I did. I thought you wouldn't be getting home until later this afternoon?"

"I couldn't wait to see you, so I took an earlier flight."

"That was sweet—thank you," I said putting my arms around him.

"I want to talk to you about next week," his tone turned more serious.

"What's next week?" I asked with my eyes half closed.

"Our 8th year wedding anniversary."

"Really?" I squealed like a little girl with a delicious secret.

"Yep, and I want to ask you something, Kels."

"Yes, Mr. Pritchard?"

"Can we have a fresh start? I want to renew our vows and take another honeymoon. I want you to never say that you don't remember marrying me. Will you Kelsey Smith-Pritchard? Will you be my wife again?"

You sneaky rat! I thought. What a set up! I had been put through hell's fire last night so that I would be prepared for this loving gesture. It's a good thing that I finally decided to forgive and release whatever Gregory's transgressions were for good. I am so grateful that you are a God of second chances—a God of rebirth.

"Yes, Gregory. I will marry you, but only if I can change my name," I stated.

"What's wrong with Pritchard?"

"Nothing, I think it's time that we were all on the same team!" I cooed.

As we lay in the bed and kissed to seal the deal, Gregory extended both of my hands above my head, took off my old wedding set and slipped a new sparkling eternity diamond band on ring on my finger. It was gorgeous.

Thank you, Jamie. I swear they're all in cahoots.

Kelsey's Revelation

In retrospect, my accident and amnesia were a calamitous way to save lost sheep and to prevent my rage from turning into murder. All of the pieces of the puzzle have come together, forming a clear view of elements from my past and present.

I, like most of the women living today, was raised to be competitive in every area of our lives. From the boardroom to the bedroom society puts undue pressure on us to outperform, outthink, and outsmart men only to come home each night with all of our accolades longing to be held tightly and protected by them.

My desire to be married may have been marred since I did not understand how to be a wife first. Growing up without my father in the household, I never had an example of headship, and the relationship with my grandfather was not enough to prepare me for the role of wife. The feeling of being conquered by a man I was more accomplished than he was a no-no in my circles. Everything I ever saw in movies, read in women's magazines, and watched on daytime talk shows proved my point. But the world is truly wrong. The ideologies of our society had raised me to cultivate a feministic attitude; it had turned me into a Lilith. I was more focused on what I thought I was going to lose through submission that fear blinded me, and I was unable to see what I would gain. My fear caused me to not see the liberty in forgiveness or the freedom of letting go. My pride wouldn't allow me to do that; my pride wouldn't allow me to be disrespected by anyone.

Pride is a killer. It is subtle and it continually nudges you to believe only what you can immediately see, forgetting about what is promised for tomorrow. Pride blinds you and yet never quite quenches the hunger of one's own self-love. One's pride can breed self-pity, selfishness, violence, anger, and the mother of them all, pride fans the fire of control, or lack thereof. More than anything, pride makes you hate yourself. Pride was the blood flowing in my veins and the essence of my destruction.

Being controlling was rooted from in childhood. Unbeknownst to me, my mom controlled the memory of my father secretly planting the seeds of a learned behavior pattern without my knowing it. Those seeds became the roots of my fundamental nature. Even with my amnesia, I was determined to control my healing process every step of the way.

My learning the spiritual truth of submission was actually based on accepting the choice that I had made when I selected my husband. The idea of submitting to a man that was not as educated or earned more than I did was inconceivable but wasn't my problem. It's what I used as an excuse to mask the true issue. So many times, I had read that people would declare to never marry again or at all as if the state of matrimony was the problem. The problem lies in the selection of whom we choose to marry. My dilemma was in my realizing that I may have rushed to marry a man who was not mature enough for the task of being a husband.

Like most women, I assumed that Gregory would eventually grow into his maturity voluntarily. However, he, like most childish men, didn't feel the need to mature until he had to. Good men with lots of potential slip into comfort zones when "superwomen" dash to put on their superhero uniform. Finding a man who is mature enough to understand that headship simply means that they are capable of wanting to assume the responsibility of leadership in the role of a husband. It doesn't mean contributing to the household only.

Gregory considered himself a "good man" because he brought his paycheck home. A good husband understands that providing income is not enough; spending time with his wife as well as creating memories and nurturing his children must also be a priority.

Gregory's financial contributions had become a bribe to condone immature and irresponsible behavior. Dr. Jamie expressed that Gregory may have felt inept due to my financial success, which ignited an unconscious competitive reaction in the form of infidelity. Like me, Gregory had also learned to communicate through a generational pattern as well—a learned behavior that had grown expectable within his family bloodline. A learned behavior pattern that I did not want my children to develop. Gregory had been bred to be habitually unfaithful to me because he had seen his father do it to his mother, and grandfather to grandmother. Or was his error the consequence of his father not being mature enough to conqueror his own demons?

True headship offers a place of equality through love. As taught on the tape in my car, husbands are commanded to "…love your wives as their own bodies; he who loves his wife loves himself." One who treasures themselves could never mistreat, deceive, or betray their wife. Most of all, it is important for a man and woman to both realize that, once married their bodies are no longer their property, but belong to their spouse. One who marries needs to understand that they are leaving their family and the family's ideologies to build one with their spouse. That doesn't mean that families should be disregarded, yet what one leaves behind is the immature ideologies and youthful habits that will distract him/her from their spouse and the family. Like Dr. Jamie, families and friends should be there to lovingly assist a married couple whenever possible.

I somehow believed that by forgiving Gregory I would lose control. I had lived a lifetime trusting only in my own abilities, raising the bar too high for others, and never letting people fall or rise to the occasion. I was fine with allowing *Gregory to wear the pants just as long as I was able to zip them up!* It was safer for me to run and hide instead of submitting to the newfound wisdom I was being taught from my inspirational tapes. When I discovered that in order to truly love my husband, I had to renew my mind, and most importantly, renew my attitude towards him, I was unwilling to do so until I thought

I knew the complete truth. Of course, this was another attempt to control. But the true state of forgiveness, which is a level of humility, is strength *under* control.

For almost four years, I negatively regarded Gregory's name, which means "watchful," as being smothering. The truth of the matter is that a husband's role *is* to be "watchful," a protector carefully guarding against anything that may harm the wife he has selected. In my foolishness, I've become stuck on the command of "…seeing that you respect your husbands." I was so busy toiling with the question of why men weren't ordered to respect wives as well. I was so distracted that I didn't realize that love is surrender, it is sacrifice, and most of all love, true love, is the highest form of respect. All of the tears shed were to water a brighter future for my husband, my babies, and myself. Don't get me wrong, I realize that Gregory is not perfect and never will be. But I can love him and myself enough to forgive but I will never forget this process. That's right I said it. Society constantly wants to teach us that we are less than a good person if we couldn't "forgive and forget." Yet, if we forget everything we have forgiven ourselves and others for, where is our testimony? Not forgetting how to forgive others and our trials allows us to choose how to develop healthy relationships. Besides, wasn't it the forgetting that got me into this mess in the first place?

So, I must start with what I have learned and move towards a brighter day of loving myself, my God, man, and my babies. The "*I can do it by myself and for myself*" ideology is a lie. The real strength in a married woman is when she can see that she has a man who supports her in every area of her life. Gregory taking care of me for the last four years has proved that he has matured and that he knows how and wants to be a husband. He is a man that will stand by me through thick and thin. This ordeal has made me feel more secure in understanding that Gregory has grown to understand and accept me even with all of my imperfections as I have to accept his.

As Gregory puts his arms around me, and we stare out into the gentle breeze of the Caribbean night's air, I'm happy with my choice.

I'm happy that we have created wedding and honeymoon memories that I will never forget. I finally feel confident that I've become one with my husband. I'm confident in knowing that I am Kelsey Pritchard. I had been holding on to a name that my mom concocted from an explicative which separated my identity from my children. I'm proud to be Mrs. Gregory Pritchard, even though I can't remember how I got here the first time; I'm proud to know I didn't lose myself totally but instead gained the love of a wonderful imperfect man. Together we are one, and together we can do anything. As I stare up into the clear dark sky filled with stars, I quietly meditate on a pearl of wisdom I now hold dear in my heart "...*that we should no longer be children, tossed to and fro and carried about with every wind of doctrine, by the trickery of men, in the cunning craftiness of deceitful plotting, but speaking the truth in love may grow up in all things...*"

Never rebuke the process of maturity.
Believe that nothing is left to chance.
If you learned it, it was for you to live it.

–LT Ladino

Upcoming Offerings from
The To and Fro Trilogy Book Series

The To and Fro Trilogy: The Wise Woman Builds

After four long years of being unsuccessful in regaining her memory, Kelsey picks up the pieces of her life and attempts to move forward. By shedding the pain of the past, Kelsey decides to forgive herself, and those closest to her, cultivating healthy relationships with her mother Kerri-Claire, her husband Gregory, and her best friend, Dr. Jamie Hyman.

The second installment provides a glimpse into Kelsey Pritchard's exodus into wedded bliss, and the return to Smith-Pritchard & Associates, her failing legal empire.

The To and Fro Trilogy: Bring Me My David

Kelsey's world is brought to a pivotal halt as she loses hope in herself and love. With so many areas of her life broken, how can Kelsey be genuinely happy for those closest to her when they find true happiness? The final installment from *The To and Fro Trilogy* further explores how to identify what happiness is versus what it may look like.

The Wise Woman Builds

Excerpt:

I cannot believe this is happening to me again! I trusted you even when I didn't trust myself. I looked to you even when I already knew all the answers. And in the end, I knew what I wanted to do but wasn't sure I was capable of going through it. I'm so pissed right now. I'm pissed that I am stuck in this situation and pissed that there's little I can do about it at the moment.

As I watch Gregory sleeping soundly next to me, I'm so angry that I was tempted to go through with one of the most unspeakable thoughts that are now percolating in my head. How can I continue to live like this? And after all we've been through in the last couple of years. Does Gregory not think about my feelings? After all, I am having his baby. Does he not care what the ramifications of his continual careless acts of inappropriate behavior will do to our children? How will it shape their character? Am I meant to constantly live with continuous marital struggles? I silently continued my tirade with tears streaming down my face and with my head clogged with images of murder. The smug look on Gregory's face made me want to look around our bedroom for a blunt object. Gregory had been asleep for almost an hour but suddenly stretched then rolled from his side onto his stomach placing his sweaty paws on me. I almost puked. I quickly slipped my body from underneath his clutches and went into the bathroom, picking up the phone and cradling it to my ear. It would be best that he does not wake up right now, or the both of us would be sorry.

"I'm still young, you know! I can do twenty-five years for murder, come out still looking good, meet another man, and quickly move on with my life!" I ranted.

"I know you're upset, Kelsey, but you have to calm down for the sake of the baby. You have every right to be upset right now, but you have to remember that every emotion you feel, so can she."

"I don't care if she can feel how upset I am. Maybe it would be good to have someone on my side for a change!"

"Why do you think I'm not on your side?"

"BECAUSE YOU ALWAYS STICK UP FOR GREGORY!" I yelled.

"That's not true at all and you know it. I just said you have every right to be upset but that doesn't give you permission to act like a fool."

"I'm not the fool, HE IS!" I accused.

"You're right, Kelsey, he is a fool, but there are ways of handling situations like this. I hope you will be woman enough to pull yourself together even in the midst of all of this. You have a big case you must defend in the morning. You have to get up and get the boys ready for school. And most of all, Kelsey, you have to act as if nothing is wrong until you are instructed as to how to handle this situation."

"Well, that's not too hard to figure out." I said defiantly, "I want a divorce!"

"That's out of the question, Kelsey. Remember for better or worse? No bailing out every time things get a little sticky," my Mentor calmly stated.

"Since he's not capable of being trusted, divorce is actually the *only* answer," I replied.

LYRICAL PRESS BOOKS are published by

Kensington Publishing Corp.
119 West 40th Street
New York, NY 10018

All Kensington titles, imprints, and distributed lines are available at special quantity discounts for bulk purchases for sales promotion, premiums, fund-raising, educational, or institutional use.

Special book excerpts or customized printings can also be created to fit specific needs. For details, write or phone the office of the Kensington Sales Manager: Kensington Publishing Corp., 119 West 40th Street, New York, NY 10018. Attn. Sales Department. Phone: 1-800-221-2647.

Lyrical Press and Lyrical Press logo Reg. U.S. Pat. & TM Off.

First Electronic Edition: November 2016
eISBN-13: 978-1-60183-899-5
eISBN-10: 1-60183-899-9

First Print Edition: November 2016
ISBN-13: 978-1-60183-902-2
ISBN-10: 1-60183-902-2

Printed in the United States of America